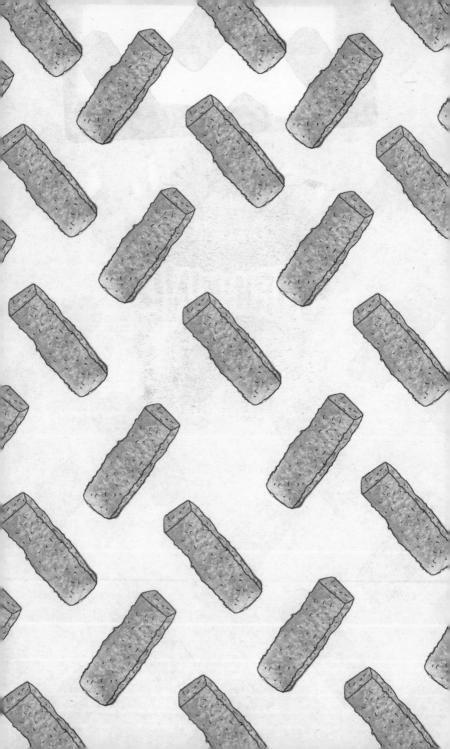

LOU KUENZLER was brought up on a remote sheep farm on the edge of Dartmoor. After a childhood of sheep, ponies, chickens and dogs, Lou moved to Northern Ireland to study theatre. She went on to work professionally as a theatre director, university drama lecturer and workshop leader in communities, schools and colleges. Lou now teaches adults and children how to write stories and is lucky enough to write her own books, too. She has written children's rhymes, plays and novels as well as stories for CBeebies. Lou lives in London with her family, two cats and a dog.

THE INCREDIBLE SHRINKING GIRL

LOU KUENZLER

Illustrated by Kirsten Collier

SCHOLASTIC

To Rachel – small but never shrinking –
thanks for everything. LK

Scholastic Children's Books
An imprint of Scholastic Ltd
Euston House, 24 Eversholt Street, London, NW1 1DB, UK
Registered office: Westfield Road, Southam, Warwickshire, CV47 0RA
SCHOLASTIC and associated logos are trademarks and/or
registered trademarks of Scholastic Inc.

First published in the UK as *Shrinking Violet* by Scholastic Ltd, 2012
This edition published 2018

Text copyright © Lou Kuenzler, 2012
Cover illustrations © Risa Rodil, 2018
Inside illustrations copyright © Kirsten Collier, 2012

The right of Lou Kuenzler and Kirstin Collier to be identified as the
author and illustrator of this work has been asserted by them.

ISBN 978 1407 18151 6

A CIP catalogue record for this book
is available from the British Library.

Printed by CPI Group (UK) Ltd, Croydon, CR0 4YY
Papers used by Scholastic Children's Books are made
from wood grown in sustainable forests.

1 3 5 7 9 10 8 6 4 2

www.scholastic.co.uk

CHAPTER 1

My name is Violet Potts.

This story begins on a **BIG** day for me. (At least, I hoped it would be a big day...) I was trying to measure how tall I was.

It was April. One whole month since my tenth birthday and I was hoping I had grown a bit since then. It's not that I'm short – I'm one of the tallest girls in class – it's just that I needed to be a few teeny-tiny centimetres TALLER.

Have you ever tried measuring yourself on your own? It's not an easy thing to do. I twisted

1

my head round, trying to read the measuring stick on the wall behind me.

"Yes!" It really looked as if I had grown!

I b..°..u..ⁿ..c...e...d around the half of the bedroom that I'm allowed to bounce around. The half that doesn't belong to my sulky fourteen-year-old sister, Tiffany-the-terrible-teenager. The half that isn't hung with more mirrors than a fancy hair salon.

"*Line*," sighed Tiffany, peering into one of the mirrors to examine a **HUGE** pink pimple on the end of her nose. "Don't you dare cross *The Line*, Violet!"

"The Line" is an old dressing-gown cord which Tiffany stapled to the floor to keep me out of her half of the room. As if I'd want to go over there anyway! Normally, I'd have listed the top ten million reasons why I have no interest whatsoever in going over to Tiffany's side.

But today was not a day to argue about room sharing. Today, I would have to be *nice*. Super-nice – because I needed Tiffany's help.

"You couldn't just pop over here and double-check *exactly* how tall I am, could you?" I asked nicely. I held out a blue crayon. If I really was as tall as I *hoped* I was, today was about to be the **BIGGEST** and BEST day of my whole life!

But Tiffany ignored me and began to squeeze her spot.

"Please!" I begged.

"No," grunted Tiffany.

"Pretty please!"

"**NO!**"

This went on for seven and a half minutes. In the end (after I offered to do ten extra washing-up duties, clean our hamster cage six times and give Tiffany two pounds and ninety-three pence), she agreed to help.

"You're exactly one point four metres tall," she said, marking a blue **V** for Violet against the measuring stick. "Are you totally, totally sure?"

I was bouncing again. "This is $HUGE$ news!"

I bounced over to one of Tiffany's million-trillion mirrors.

"*Line*," she squealed, but I ignored her and took a good look at myself. I looked pretty much the same as usual. The same short brown hair. Same skinny arms and freckly nose... But I *was* a little taller. Now I looked closely, I could *DEFINITELY* see it. My favourite dark purple dungarees were short above my ankles now.

"So you've grown. What's the big deal?" sighed Tiffany.

Sisters can be so stupid sometimes!

"The big deal is exactly that!" I said. "I am BIG at last. I am one point four metres tall. That means I am legally, lawfully, totally tall enough to ride on PLUNGER!"

"Plunger?" sniffed Tiffany. "Not that stupid roller coaster thing?"

I couldn't believe what I was hearing. I love scary theme-park rides. The bigger and scarier the better.

"PLUNGER! is NOT *stupid!*" I fumed. "PLUNGER! is awesome! PLUNGER! is the BIGGEST, FASTEST, most FEARSOME roller-coaster ride in the whole country!"

"Whatever!" Tiffany flopped back on to her bed. "I don't know why you're so excited. You'll never get to go on it anyway."

But that's where Tiffany was wrong. Dad had promised he would take me, just as soon as I was tall enough.

CHAPTER 2

A week later, our whole family stood in the queue to ride PLUNGER!

Dad had made his promise and he had to stick to it.

"I can't believe it!" I cried, turning cartwheels in the line and nearly kicking the woman behind us in the face.

"Sorry!" I said. "It's just that this is AMAZING!"

I'd been on loads of scary rides before – at the fairground and things – but never anything as FAST and HUGE as PLUNGER!

"It does look *very* big," said Mum.

We all stared up at the roller coaster. It was by far the tallest ride in the theme park, towering above everything else. Its shiny tracks twisted up high into the sky, then plunged back down to the ground. It looked as if an ENORMOUS GIANT was practising huge curly handwriting in the sky.

"I don't know how you talked us into this,

Violet," said Mum. Her face had gone a funny green cabbagey colour.

"It's going to be **BRILLIANT!**" I said. "We'll be hurled through the air so fast, we'll throw up that horrible Oaty Flake cereal we had for breakfast!"

"And that's a good thing?" asked Dad, looking up from a text he was sending.

"We'll die of boredom first!" groaned Tiffany as the queue edged slowly forward. "I can't believe I've had to wait *all* morning for this!"

"You're lucky," I told her. "I've had to wait my WHOLE life!"

It's true. I've been desperate to ride on PLUNGER! ever since I was tiny. Even before I could read, I pointed to a picture of the roller coaster in a library book called *One Thousand Scary Things To Do Before You Die!* I made Dad borrow a copy and read to me about the roller coaster every night.

Now we were almost there! If only the queue would move faster.

Dad checked the emails on his phone. Tiffany squeezed a new pimple on the end of her nose.

Mum closed her eyes and tried to meditate.

"Ommmmmmmmmmmmm! Think of a calm place," she hummed. "A beautiful beach. No roller coasters, just palm trees and sand. Ommmmmm..."

"Can we have a fizzy drink while we wait?" I asked.

"No!" Mum didn't even blink. "Ommmmmmm! Fizzy drinks are..."

"...**JUST JUNK!**" chorused me and Tiffany together. Mum's super-strict about junk food and healthy eating. Which was pretty funny, actually, because right now her face was as green as all the green vegetables she has ever made us eat!

"But Dad's got a fizzy drink," said Tiffany.

"No I haven't." Dad looked down at the giant cup he was holding. "This is ... er ... just water. We're nearly there now, anyway. Look!"

At last, the entrance was in sight. A carriage full of screaming passengers thundered over our heads. I could see people's wide-open mouths, their cheeks pulled back by the force of the wind, their hair flying upside down as they bombed, head first, towards the ground.

"WICKED!"

"Ommmmmmmmmm!" said Mum, screwing her eyes tight shut and groaning louder than ever.

I looked at the sign up ahead, and the big red measuring line, which said:

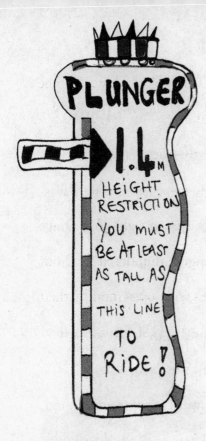

PLUNGER

▶1.4ₘ

HEIGHT RESTRICTION YOU MUST BE AT LEAST AS TALL AS THIS LINE TO RIDE!

"Are you *sure* you measured me properly, Tiff?" I said.

"Of course I measured you properly." Tiffany turned away in a huff. She was probably right. Dad had measured me too ... and Mum ... and Gran ... and the school nurse ... even a man with a tape measure in the DIY store.

"There's nothing to worry about!" I agreed. "I am *EXACTLY* one point four metres tall!"

But the minute I stepped up to the measuring line, I knew something was wrong.

Wrong . . . and wobbly . . . and WEIRD!

All my excitement seemed to EXPLODE inside me like a bomb. My toes tingled. There was a sudden dizzy feeling as if I was going to faint. Then a lurch in the pit of my stomach. . .

WHOOSH!

It felt as if I was riding PLUNGER! already – although I hadn't even left the queue yet.

I was plummeting towards the ground! Wind whistled past my ears. There was a juddering in my bones.

Other people's shoulders, arms, legs, knees whooshed by – a blur of colour – as I shot down towards the ground.

Down... Down... Down...

High above me I could see the clear red mark of the measuring line, marking the spot where the top of my head had been just a moment earlier.

"Stop!" I cried.

But I went hurtling on.

I was plunging downwards.

I was shrinking! Fast!

CHAPTER 3

I have **NEVER**, *EVER* screamed on a scary ride –

not even at the fairground when the big wheel got

stuck with me right at the top. But I screamed now.

I screamed as hard and loud as I could...

"Ahhhhhhhhhhhhhhhhh!"

I tried to grab hold of the top of Mum's boot

as I whizzed by. I was shrinking so fast, my ears

popped, like they do on an aeroplane.

Then, with one last lurch, it was over. The

sinking feeling stopped. My legs crumpled beneath

me and I fell flat on my back, my head spinning...

Yikes! As I sat up, a giant snake wriggled past me on the edge of the path. It was twice as long as I was – like a **MASSIVE PYTHON!**

It took me a moment to realize it was only an earthworm.

Everything around me seemed **HUGE**. The long grass was like a thick jungle and every pebble like a rock. Three ants the size of tigers marched past. I scrambled to my feet and peered up from beneath a giant dock leaf that was like one of those big cafe umbrellas above my head.

High, high above me, Dad was still fiddling with his phone.

"Where's Violet gone?" he said. His voice sounded as if he was shouting down a long, windy tunnel. "She was standing right beside me a moment ago."

Mum stopped humming. She opened her eyes and looked around too. "Violet? Where are you?"

"I'm down here!" I cried, jumping up and waving my little matchstick arms in the air. How could this have happened? I wasn't supposed to shrink! I was supposed to be one point four metres tall. . . Now I was no bigger than a frozen fish finger!

"HELP!" I hollered. But my voice was as tiny as I was.

Mum and Dad and Tiff didn't seem to hear me. They were *so* far above – like giants. **HUGE** giants, who could crush me with a single step.

"LOOK OUT!" I dodged one of Dad's enormous feet – my head was level with the top of his trainers.

"I bet Violet ducked under the railings," said Tiffany. "I bet she was too scared to go on the ride after all! What a baby!"

"I may be small," I roared, "but I am NOT a baby!"

It was scary to have shrunk so fast. I had no idea why it had happened ... and no idea if I'd *ever* grow tall again. But I wasn't going to cry. No matter what Tiffany said about me. No matter if I never even got to ride on PLUNGER!

Violet Potts does not cry! Violet Potts is NOT a baby!

At least the clothes I was wearing had shrunk with me, otherwise I'd have had to make myself an outfit out of leaves or something. I looked down at my tiny doll-size jeans and sweater. I remembered how Tiffany's favourite blue top had shrunk in the wash. She'd cried for a whole afternoon. Now that's what I call a real baby!

"Typical Violet to disappear," Tiffany moaned. "She never does what she's told." I leapt sideways as she almost speared me with her high-heeled shoe. (Who wears high heels to a theme park, for goodness' sake?)

"Come on!" said Mum. "We'll have to go and look for her!"

"Wait!" I cried, scrambling on to Dad's trainer. I clung to his laces for dear life as he strode away from the queue.

"Violet's in big trouble when we do find her!" he said.

"It's so unfair!" moaned Tiffany. "We didn't even get to go on the roller coaster."

Her long, skinny legs stomped past, wearing a miniskirt high above her knobbly knees. "Stop complaining, Stork Legs!" I shouted. "You never even wanted to go on the ride in the first place!"

"I could have been shopping with Monique

this morning," she whined. "She was going to get her ears pierced and I was going to—"

"Where *is* Violet?" Mum sounded really worried now. "She could be anywhere. Theme parks are very dangerous places, you know."

Too right! At that moment, Dad stumbled on a stone and I was hurled forward. His back shoe (the one I was riding on) smashed into the front one like a bumper car at full speed. I slammed down hard and thumped my chin against the big, tight knot in Dad's laces.

"Ow!" This place really *was* dangerous! A walk up the path was more like a roller-coaster ride for me! Like riding PLUNGER! might be. Only now, there was no safety harness and I was DANGEROUSLY *small!*

"I'll go to the Lost Child Tent," said Mum. "You stay and look around here, Stuart."

"Right-ho!" said Dad. "Call me on the mobile if you find her."

"Tiffany, you check the ladies' toilets." Mum set off at a sprint. Tiffany headed off pretty fast, too ... probably because she remembered there'd be mirrors in the toilet.

I clung on tightly to Dad's shoe. He stood still, scanning the theme park. I could see the sun glinting off his specs.

"Violet," he called. "If this is one of your jokes, it is <u>not</u> funny."

I do like jokes. Just yesterday, I'd put a plastic fried egg on Dad's laptop. You should have seen his face when he thought there'd be yolk on the keyboard. But now I was tiny, there was no way I was going to muck around. If I got split up from Dad now I'd be lost in the theme park for ever. I might be trampled underfoot, run over by a buggy or drowned in a puddle.

"I'M DOWN HERE!" I yelled, for the hundredth time. My throat was starting to hurt, but it was no good. He still couldn't hear me.

I'll have to climb up, I thought. *He'll be able to hear me if I shout right down his ear.*

I've had plenty of practice at climbing. I'm always playing on the spider's web at the adventure playground in our park. The soft cotton of Dad's trousers was much easier to grip than the scratchy nylon rope I was used to. I pulled myself upwards, hand over hand, as I shim_mied uP Dad's leg. Then I clung to a belt loop on his waist.

"Whoo!" It's a good job I'm not scared of heights. It was a long way back down!

It was still a long way up too! I'd need to haul myself up Dad's jacket like a rock climber. I'd have to scramble all the way to his shoulder and shout into his ear from there.

Unless I could hitch a ride. I watched as Dad took a slurp of his drink. If only I could jump on to his cup when he lowered it. The next time he lifted it to take a sip, I'd be staring him in the face. He'd have to notice me then!

I balanced my feet on the top of Dad's belt, spreading my arms as if I were leaping on to the zip-wire at King's Park.

Dad's arm whooshed past me as he lifted the cup.

"Geronimo!" I threw myself into the air. For a moment I was flying. Then I caught hold of the bendy straw with both hands, clinging on to it like a rung on the monkey bars.

"Yes!" I swung my feet down on to the rim of the paper cup. I'd done it! I was balancing on the edge of Dad's drink like a tightrope walker.

I held my head high (or as high as I could), threw back my shoulders and spread out my arms like aeroplane wings. (Like tiny toy aeroplane wings, at least!)

But just at that moment, Dad shot forward. "Excuse me!" he called out. I was thrown SOMERSAULTING into the air as he ran up to a theme park lady in a yellow jacket. "I've lost my daughter. Can you help?"

I only just managed to catch hold of the rim of the cup, my fingers slipping on the damp, shiny paper as I fell.

"She's got freckles and short brown hair," said Dad. "And she's about this tall." He held out his hand to measure my height – the height I *used* to be – just above his elbow.

"Hold up your thumb, Dad," I called, dangling on the inside of the cup. "That's more the size I am now."

"Where did you last see her?" asked the theme park lady.

My feet were hanging dangerously close to the ice-filled water beneath me.

"We were in the queue for the roller coaster," said Dad. "She loves scary rides. . ."

"But not THIS scary," I squealed as Dad waved his drink in the air again. Who'd have thought a cup ride could be the SCARIEST thing in the theme park. Scarier even than PLUNGER! perhaps?

"We were standing right there!" Dad sloshed his drink forward as he pointed towards the queue.

My fingers slipped. I felt the rim of the cup slide through my grip.

"Ahhhhhhhhhhhhhhhhh!"

Down I plunged. Down into the deep, cold liquid below.

CHAPTER 4

SPLOSH!

I was winded by the shock of the freezing water.

No! Not water!

Gasping, I swam to the surface of the cup, my nose full of bubbles and my mouth full of . . . LEMONADE! That was SO unfair! Dad had said his drink was "only water"! I dived down for another sip.

Normally, I'd have finished the lot. I LOVE lemonade! But now, after just three gulps, my tiny tummy was bulging. I felt bloated and full of enormous bubbles. The lemonade was freezing and my legs began to ache from paddling against the rising fizz.

I tried to push up and grab the edge of the cup. But the rim was just out of reach. I scrabbled against the steep white sides, like the slippery walls of a giant swimming pool.

A huge ice cube – it looked about twice as big as my head – bobbed sideways and thumped me in the chest. Down I went, plunging towards the bottom of the cup.

D
   o
      w
        n

d

    o

       w

          n

            d

              o

                w

                  n.

I remembered a picture I'd seen in a literacy lesson at school ... of the *Titanic* – the big ship – sinking into the ocean after it had hit an iceberg.

Now I know how it feels, I thought.

As my foot hit the bottom of the cup, I kicked hard, pushing myself up.

I could drown, I thought, swimming towards

the light. *I could drown in Dad's drink.*

At last I came to the surface, gasping for air. My hair was plastered to my head, sticky with lemonade.

"DAD!" I called out, desperately trying to keep my head above the bubbles. "DAD! HELP ME, PLEASE!"

But it was hopeless. My little shout was blotted out by the sounds of screaming and the clattering wheels of the roller coaster above my head.

I tried to tread water, like I'd learned in swimming lessons. But me and my best friend, Nisha, always muck about during that bit. We think it's boring. We pretend to drop our goggles so we can dive down to the bottom of the pool. Nisha pretends she's a mermaid. I pretend I'm a shark!

But I didn't want to dive now. I didn't have the

strength. I could barely keep my arms moving. My tiny fingers felt like slivers of ice. And I couldn't even feel my toes.

High above me I heard the theme park lady's voice. "Follow me, sir," she said to Dad. "Let's go back to the queue and look for your daughter there."

"Good idea!" agreed Dad. His cup jerked –

lemonade . . . swirled . . . whirlpool . . . around . . . me . . . like . . . a . . .

I spun in circles. A jet of liquid shot out of

the cup.

I was carried with
it, flying through
the air as if I were
shooting off the
end of a super-fast
water ride. With a big
wet *SQUELCH*, I hit
something soft beneath me.

The cup bounced away. Lemonade sploshed on
to my head.

Where am I? What just happened?

Dazed, I looked up and saw iron mesh all around me. I tried to struggle to my feet, but slipped on a giant slice of tomato. The smell of rotten hamburger filled my nose.

I was in a litter bin!

Dad had thrown his cup away! ... And he'd thrown me away too!

"Wait!" I clambered on to a half-eaten burger bun. The bread felt SOFT and SPRINGY beneath my feet, like a giant trampoline.

If I lost sight of Dad, I'd never find him again. Without him, I'd never be able to get home. It would take me a week just to reach the exit of the theme park.

"COME BACK, DAD! DON'T LEAVE ME!" I bounced

up and down waving my arms, shouting through the criss-crossed wire sides of the bin.

But Dad kept on walking. He followed the theme park lady as she led him back towards the PLUNGER! queue.

"Stop!" I cried helplessly as he disappeared into the crowd.

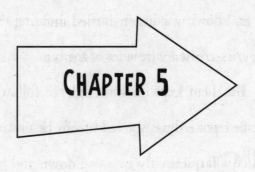

CHAPTER 5

"Watch out! There's a child in this bin!" I cried as a woman tossed a half-finished cup of strawberry milkshake away and hurried on past. The thick pink liquid splashed over me like the BIGGEST, WETTEST, STICKIEST wave machine ever.

"Yuck!"

I dodged sideways but was hit from behind by a shower of popcorn raining down like giant balls in a ball pit.

"Doesn't anybody ever finish their food?" I yelped as half a hot dog followed.

By now I was nearly buried under dark and dingy litter. It was like being lost in a giant haunted house or theme park spooky castle.

As I poked my head out from behind a chip packet, a fat, shiny fly swooped down and landed on me. Its huge hairy bum covered my face as it slurped pink milk from my hair like a VAMPIRE BAT...

"Yuck! Buzz off!"

The fly flapped away, looking surprised.

Something big rustled inside a pizza box beside me.

Was it a rat? Mum says rats are always sniffing in bins looking for scraps.

"Just stay where you are!" I said to the whatever-it-was.

I'd seen the size of flies compared to me... If they were like bats, a rat would be like a horse. Or a dinosaur ... a TYRANNOSAURUS RAT! No thank you. I wasn't hanging around for that.

The pizza box rustled again.

I leapt on to the wire mesh round the side of the bin and began to climb towards the top. As I glanced back, I thought I saw a black beady eye looking up at me.

The sharp wire dug into my hands. I tried to get a foothold in each little triangle of mesh as I scrambled higher and higher.

Charlie Hudson in my class had a climbing wall party last term. I went right to the very top where only grown-ups are supposed to go. But then, I had a harness on ... and an instructor ...

and the climbing wall wasn't covered in slimy hamburger grease.

"Whoops!" My hand slipped. I lost my grip and almost tumbled right back down into the pit of flies (and possibly giant TyRATosaurus) below.

"I've really got to get out of here!" I groaned, swinging helplessly by one arm. "I've got to get back to Mum and Dad."

CHAPTER 6

I had a good grip again and climbed about halfway
up the wire mesh of the litter bin when I spotted
Mum running down the path.

She was sprinting back towards PLUNGER!,
calling my name. "Violet? Violet? Where are you?"
Her face wasn't as green as a cabbage any more – it
was as white as a rice cake (another of her favourite
healthy foods, as it happens). She was dodging
in and out of the crowd, trying to spot me in the
throng. Just as she came level with the litter bin,
she stopped. For a split second, I thought she'd seen

me. My heart was pounding – its small solid thud drumming against my tiny chest.

"MUM!" I cried.

But she'd only stopped to shout at Dad down her mobile phone.

"Stuart? Any luck at the roller coaster? ... The Lost Child Tent haven't seen her either. They're going to put out an announcement... There it is now. Can you hear it?"

A high-pitched, tinny voice which almost split my eardrums boomed across the theme park:

WOULD LOST CHILD VIOLET POTTS PLEASE COME TO THE MISSING PERSON'S TENT BY THE ENTRANCE GATES. YOUR MUM AND DAD ARE VERY WORRIED ABOUT YOU. THAT'S VIOLET POTTS, TO COME TO THE MISSING PERS...

Over the sound of the announcement, I heard another loud voice. Much closer. "Shall I empty this one, Len?"

"Might as well, Glen."

I looked up to see a big black rubber glove looming down towards me.

Len and Glen were LITTER BIN MEN! One of them was pushing a cart – the sort of cart they empty litter bins into . . . right before they take all the litter to be chewed up in a dustbin lorry . . . or crushed by a giant steam roller . . . or tossed and sorted by an enormous grabber claw.

Whatever it is they do with theme park litter, it wasn't going to be good. Not for a teeny-tiny girl who'd shrunk to the size of a chocolate bar wrapper. I'd just clambered over one of those small fun-size ones. Well there's nothing fun about being this size – let me tell you that. Not when Glen and Len, the Killer Bin Men, are about to empty you into their *CART OF DOOM!*

"Sorry!" said Mum, stepping out of their way. Trust her to be polite even in a moment of total panic. With that she was off. Charging away to look for me by the hot dog stand or something.

Glen – I think he was the one with the moustache – grabbed hold of the litter bin and heaved it on to his shoulder.

"Watch out!"

I felt my fingers slipping. . .

"Noooooo!"

I was plunging downwards. . .

SQUELCH!

I landed flat on my back, amongst the half-chewed burgers once again.

This time I saw it! The rat – and it was the size of a DINOSAUR! The huge beast leapt out of its pizza box and up on to the wire, thrashing its scaly tail. One, two, three leaps (I had to admire its speed and jumping skill) and the brute was out of the bin. It scurried away into the same block of toilets where I'd seen Tiffany disappear earlier. . . She couldn't *still* be in there, could she?

"D'you see that?" cried Len.

"It's run right into the ladies' toilets!" gasped Glen.

A moment later Tiffany came charging out of the door screaming her head off.

"A rat!" she squealed. "Now I've dropped my eyeliner pencil down the drain!"

I don't know if it was the shock of the rat, or my helpless laughter as I watched Tiffany run screaming across the grass – but something inside me went POP!

A second later, there I was. Back to full size. Sitting wedged inside the litter bin.

CHAPTER 7

Dad started the car.

"I've never been so embarrassed in my whole life!" said Mum. "What on earth made you want to hide in a litter bin, Violet?"

"I wasn't hiding!" I said. "I told you. I was—"

"Three men it took to cut you out of there!" said Dad. He wound down the electric windows and shook the little fir-tree air freshener hanging from the mirror in the car. "That smell of rotten hamburger is disgusting!"

"Junk food!" sniffed Mum, as if this explained

it all.

"I still don't see why we have to leave the theme park," I said as Dad reversed out of the car park. "I never even got to ride on PLUNGER!"

"Ha!" snorted Tiffany. "You might have got to ride on it, if you hadn't run away!"

"I didn't run away!"

"It's all right that you were frightened," said Mum.

"I wasn't frightened!"

Mum ignored this. "I was frightened too, darling. Lunger. . ."

" PLUNGER!"

" PLUNGER! did look very big! If I were as little as you are. . ."

"But I *wasn't* as little as I am!" I explained for

the hundredth time. "I was much, much, much littler! I was the same size as. . ."

"As this?" said Tiffany, taking a lipstick out of her bag and waving it under my nose. "You've already told us, Violet! We just don't believe you, that's all!"

She tossed the lipstick back in her handbag and pulled out a bottle of sickly-sweet bubblegum perfume, which she sprayed all over the car. "You were scared. You hid in a bin. Your bum was too big to get out again. And now you stink. End of story!"

"Tiffany!" said Dad. "You're not helping."

I picked a slice of squashed tomato off my sleeve and thought about dropping it down the back of Tiffany's neck. But that would only make

Mum and Dad even more mad at me. So, I decided to be nice and threw it out of the window for the birds to eat.

"PLEASE can we go back?" I begged. I was scared I might shrink again, but it was worth it if I could try to ride on PLUNGER! one more time.

"I'll stay right beside you, Mum. I'll even hold your hand if it'll make you change your mind!"

"Afraid not!" said Dad, setting the satnav for home. He knows the way perfectly well, but he loves to fiddle with gadgets. "I've had quite enough of theme parks for one day." he said as drove out through the gates.

"But can we come back tomorrow?" I said, twisting in my seat to try and catch a last glimpse of PLUNGER! "Please? I'm begging you really nicely! Please, please, PLEASE?"

"We won't be coming back here for a *very* long time," said Mum sternly. "This was your treat, Violet. But you ruined it for all of us. I don't mind that you got lost. I suppose that could have happened to anybody. What I do mind is the lies you told."

"I didn't tell lies!"

"All this nonsense about shrinking!" said Mum, as Dad pulled on to the main road. "That's what's made us really cross, Violet."

"But—"

"I don't want to hear another word about it! *Ever.* Do you understand me?"

"It's not fair!" I pushed my nose against the car window, hiding the tears welling up in my eyes.

How could they not believe me?

But now everything was back to normal, I almost didn't believe it myself. After all, people don't just shrink . . . do they?

"Anyway," said Mum cheerily, "now that we're leaving the theme park early, we'll have time to visit Grandma."

"Typical!" said Tiffany. "I *still* don't get to go shopping. But I have to spend the whole afternoon in an old folks' home."

After that, no one spoke very much at all. Tiffany put her headphones in. Mum closed her eyes and listened to the meditation CD she'd put on the stereo.

Imagine you're a cloud … a light, fluffy, carefree cloud.

"At least clouds don't have children who get lost in theme parks!" chuckled Dad as we turned on to the motorway.

He was trying to be funny, but Mum ignored him. I didn't laugh either. It was no joke that I'd missed my chance to ride on PLUNGER!

I stared out of the window, questions buzzing in my head.

Why had I shrunk? Why had I unshrunk? Would I ever shrink again?

And, if I *did* shrink, *when* would it happen next?

CHAPTER 8

Gran lives at the Sunset Retirement Centre. It's a brilliant place for old people who are still fit and healthy, but there are nurses there to look after them if they need it. I wish she could come and live with us. But we don't have enough bedrooms and I already have to share with Tiffany. **WORST LUCK!**

As soon as we arrived at the centre, Mum and Dad went round the back to see the new garden that's just been finished. There's a big flat lawn so the old folks can do special, gentle yoga and t'ai chi to help them stay fit. Mum says it's really important for old folks to stay active and lively if they can.

Tiffany went to see the garden too. Only because she fancies one of the gardeners. But I ran on inside to grab a couple of minutes on my own with Gran. Now she really *is* lively! Although she gets pain in her bones sometimes, she's always full of energy: learning to ballroom dance, doing archery and playing ping-pong. She says if she lives to be a hundred she'll celebrate by swimming the English Channel. I bet she would too – wearing her favourite, crazy swimming costume with pink flamingos all over it.

"Violet!" she grinned as soon as she saw me.

One of the things I love most about Gran is the lines round her eyes. They look like crinkly crisps. She says they make her look old, but they come from laughing so much.

"How's my favourite, smallest granddaughter?" she smiled.

"Not great, actually!" I said as I ran towards her wide-open arms. I almost tripped over Barry Bling. He's the beautician who works at the retirement centre.

He was crouched down trying to paint Gran's toenails bright purple to match the SPARKLY sequin top she was wearing.

"They call this colour Vibrant Violet!" winked Gran, wriggling her toes. "It's gorgeous! It makes me think of you."

"But your name's Violet too!" I laughed. Gran is Mum's mum and I'm named after her – it's why I have such an old-fashioned name.

"Careful!" cried Barry as I dodged past him and hugged Gran tight. Her familiar pepperminty smell washed over me.

Gran must have been sniffing me too because she giggled and said, "You smell very CLEAN, Violet. Like a Norwegian pine forest ... or a freshly scrubbed toilet floor!"

"I had a bit of . . . *trouble* at the theme park,"
I explained. We'd taken a detour home so that I
could shower and get rid of the smell of the bin.

"Mum made me wash my hair with special
pine-scented shampoo," I said. "It's supposed to kill
all known bugs and germs and—"

"HORRORS!" Barry Bling leapt to his feet. "You
don't have head lice, do you? Those shampoos never
do any good and I know what you kids are like.
Always scratching. Forever infested with something."

"I'm sure Violet hasn't got head lice. Have you,
dear?" smiled Gran.

"No!" I shook my head and Barry leapt even
further away. I think he was afraid a shower of nits
might fly out of my hair and land in his curly blond
locks. (Barry has long golden hair, all the way down

to his shoulders. I'm sure he dyes it – which is odd because it really doesn't match the colour of the orange fake-tan cream he rubs on his skin. Tiffany has some too, but she hasn't worn it since Dad said she looked like Mum's carrot juice smoothie.)

"You have to get out of here!" cried Barry. "I can't have head lice hopping around my beauty salon."

"She hasn't got head lice!" said Gran. "And this is not your beauty salon. It's *my* bedroom. All you've done is drag that thing in here!" She pointed to a gold suitcase on wheels. Barry had written across it in big, shiny letters:

BLING'S THINGS!

Hair Care and Beauty for the More Mature Client

Barry does beauty treatments for nearly all the old ladies. He comes to the centre most days to curl their hair, do facials or paint their nails. He's so busy, he often does two jobs at once.

Like now! Grumpy old Mrs Paterson, who has the room next door to Gran, popped her head round the door. One side of her hair was in tight curlers, the other hanging down in thin grey strands.

"Aren't you coming back, Barry?" she grumbled. "My hair's only half done! I have a very weak heart. I haven't got *forever* to wait around, you know."

Barry ignored her. He was leaning close to the mirror on Gran's dressing table. His shiny purple shirt was open at the neck. He was scratching the chest hair under his big gold, diamond-studded B-for-Barry necklace.

"I think I'm already infested!" he shuddered. He leant forward, scratching his chest madly and almost knocking everything off Gran's dressing table. The lamp tipped over. It clattered against the **WORLD'S BEST GRANNY** mug that I'd given her for her birthday.

"Careful!" I cried.

"Take him away, Mrs P," smiled Gran. "My toenails are done. I'll have a nice cup of tea and a quiet chat with Violet."

"Good! I'll send my grandson Riley in too," said Mrs Paterson.

"Actually," said Gran, "I thought it might be nice if Violet and I had a bit of private time before—"

"Pardon?" Mrs Paterson stuck her finger in her ear. "I don't hear properly, you know. I'll send Riley round anyway. He'll just get bored watching Barry finish my hair. If he gets jumpy, it's not good for my heart."

She disappeared into the corridor.

"There's nothing wrong with her heart," sighed Gran. "And she's not a bit deaf either. She can hear every word when she wants to."

"And now we'll have to put up with Riley Paterson!" I groaned.

Riley goes to my school … but he is not my friend.

Last term, he put stick insects in my lunch box to try and scare me. When I wasn't scared, he tried to feed the poor creatures to his Venus flytrap plant instead.

He is the **WORST** and **MEANEST** boy in my whole class!

CHAPTER 9

"Is it true, then?" said Riley, barging into Gran's room. He was trying to hide a mean little grin but his ratty nose wrinkled up all the same.

"Is *what* true?" I said, as if I didn't know what he was going to say. I'd seen him scuttling about in the car park when we first arrived. Tiffany was still moaning on and on about the *TERRIBLE* day she'd had and how it was all my FAULT!

"Is it true that you ran away from the roller-coaster ride?" Ratty-Riley grinned.

"No!" I said. "I didn't run anywhere."

"That's not what I heard your sister say!" sniggered Riley. "I heard big brave Violet Potts cried like a baby."

"I didn't cry," I said. "I just didn't fancy going on the ride, that's all." There was no way that I was going to tell him that I'd shrunk.

"Ha!" Riley's grin was huge now. He sucked air through the gap in his teeth. "I thought it was your '*life ambition*' to go on PLUNGER! That's what you said in that *boring* story you read out in class. '*If I had three wishes, I'd wish for three rides on Plunger!*,' that's what you said."

"Well, I've changed my mind," I snapped. "If I had three wishes now, I'd wish that you'd be squashed by a rhino, Riley Paterson!"

"That's only one wish!" said Riley.

He thinks he's *so clever*!

"OK, OK! I wish you'd be squashed by a rhino, chewed up by a tiger . . . and then swallowed by a shark!"

"Riley, dear," said Gran in her sweetest, most helpless old-lady voice. "Why don't you nip down to the kitchen and see if you can find us some nice biscuits. There's a good lad."

"Why me?" said Riley. "Why can't Vi—"

"See if they've got of any of those pink ones," said Gran. "You know . . . the pink wafers. They're my favourite. I've got a terrible sweet tooth!"

Riley had no choice but to go. "All right, Mrs Short," he said as Gran held out an empty saucer.

As soon as he'd gone, Gran picked up a magazine and looked at the word search puzzle. She was pretending to concentrate but I knew she was going to say something. I knew she'd got rid of Ratty-Riley on purpose.

"Of course, it's none of my business," she said at last, "but you shouldn't let him do that, you know."

"Do what?" I asked.

Gran circled a word in her puzzle. "Don't let him make you angry, Violet! Don't let him make you feel small!"

"I don't *feel* small," I said. "I just. . . It doesn't

matter." I picked at the seam on my jeans. I love Gran, but there was no point in telling her how I really felt. She'd be just like everyone else in the family. She'd either laugh at me or call me a liar. There was no point in telling her that it wasn't *feeling* small that was my problem. It was *being* small that was upsetting me. Shrinking to the same size as a **PINK-WAFER BISCUIT** to be precise.

"I do know how it is," said Gran. She put down her magazine and gently lifted my chin. "I know *exactly* how it is, pet." She tilted my head so that I had to look up at her. "Sometimes, when I was your age, I used to feel *very* small."

Gran held up her finger and wriggled it. "Sometimes I felt *tiny* – no more than a few inches tall. Fancy that. Eh?" she winked.

I stared straight into Gran's twinkling blue eyes. Was she trying to tell me something? It seemed almost as if she knew that I'd shrunk.

But that was silly. How could she know? All I'd said was that I didn't ride on PLUNGER!

Gran leant forward and squeezed my hand. "I'm glad we're having this chat, Violet. There's a little something you should know. . ."

"A *little* something?" my voice had gone quiet and croaky, almost a whisper.

"Yes," said Gran. "You see, the thing is, I—"

But just then, the door **banged** open and Riley scurried back in with a plate of custard creams. "The thing is," said Gran quickly, "I've had far too many biscuits already.

A *little* can go a *very* long way, I find. Don't you, Violet?"

"Are we really talking about biscuits, Gran?" I hissed, as Riley turned his back to gobble a custard cream. I had to ask her straight out. "Are we talking about biscuits . . . or people? TINY LITTLE PEOPLE?"

But Gran just smiled and called Riley over. "Weren't there any pink ones, dear?" she said. "I'm not very fond of custard creams."

Then, just when I thought she wouldn't say anything else, Gran turned and whispered something to me. She spoke *so* fast and *so* low that I almost didn't catch what she saying.

It was only a minute after she'd finished speaking that what she told me *actually* sank in.

"Don't worry, Violet," she whispered. "When I was your age, I was a shrinker too."

CHAPTER 10

The following Saturday, I drove Tiff mad by staying locked in the bathroom all afternoon.

"Shrink!" I commanded, staring hard at my reflection. *"Come on, Violet!* SHRINK!" It was almost exactly a week since I'd shrunk in the PLUNGER! queue. (And a week since I'd last seen Gran.) She was the only person who believed me about shrinking but we had never got to finish our conversation.

As soon as she'd told me she used to shrink too, Mum and Dad and Tiffany had come in. Tiffany was all giggly because Sean the gardener had picked her a rose.

So now I'd asked Mum if I could visit the Sunset Retirement Centre later this evening. I love having supper with the old ladies – they always have pizza or burgers on a Saturday night ... not a green vegetable in sight! More than anything, though, I wanted to spend time with Gran and hear about her shrinking adventures from long ago.

"SHRINK!" I tried again. I wriggled my toes, hoping they'd start to tingle. But still nothing happened.

I admit it, when I shrank at the theme park, I was TOTALLY FREAKED OUT! It all happened so fast – there I was, a tiny little squashable thing! I didn't think I'd ever grow back to my normal size. But now, I was desperate to give it another go. Think of all the cool things I could do if I was tiny again.

I could climb inside Mum's bedside locker. I'd secretly nibble the stash of hidden chocolate she thinks we don't know about – a single square would be like a **GIANT** family-size bar to me. (But my tooth marks would be so tiny, they'd blame it on mice!)

Then I could sneak into Tiffany's handbag and spy on her when she goes out with her friends. That would be pretty boring, actually – but I could TORTURE Tiff later, by threatening to tell Mum everything I'd seen.

And I could hide in Dad's pocket when he does

his sponsored parachute jump next week. That would be AWESOME! He does it every year with people from the computer company where he works. They skydive from an aeroplane to raise money for charity. I've been asking for *ages* if I can have a go too, but everyone always says I'm too little. Ha! Well, there's no such thing as too little if you're *so* tiny that no one even knows you're there!

The trouble is, no matter how hard I tried, I just couldn't manage to shrink again.

"COME ON!" I peered into the mirror for the hundredth time.

There must be something special that sparks the shrinking off. That was NUMBER ONE of the HUNDRED AND ONE questions I wanted to ask Gran as soon as I saw her tonight.

But, as it turned out, I didn't get the chance to ask any questions at all.

When I finally arrived at the retirement centre, the first person I saw was Riley *Raterson* – Paterson. He was stealing peanuts from the snack table in the lounge. Honestly, if he *actually* had whiskers and a tail, I'd call a rat catcher to get rid of him!

"Are you here to see your grandma?" he asked, his cheeks stuffed full of nuts. "Better make the most of it before she gets sent to PRISON!"

"Prison? Why would anyone want to send Gran to prison?"

"Because she's a thief!" said Riley. "Everyone knows it!" And with that he scuttled away.

What was he talking about? Gran wasn't a thief. But from the way Riley's grandmother and some of the other old folks in the lounge were looking at me – their noses turned up as if I'd trodden in dog poo – something odd was definitely going on.

I *SPED OFF* towards Gran's room to find out.

"Hello, Mr Gupta!" I cried as I passed him in the corridor. "Do you know where my gran is?"

Mr Gupta is ancient! He looks about six hundred and fifty years old and has hardly any teeth. But he's one of my favourite residents. Whenever he sees me, he gives me a mint humbug. (They're always covered in fluff from his pocket, but I don't care.)

Today, he didn't even offer me a sweet. He just looked worried and shook his head.

"I haven't seen your grandmother anywhere,"
he said. "But when you find her, tell her . . . tell her
I don't believe a word of it. Tell her she still has
friends in this place."

"Wait. What do you mean? Don't believe a word of *what*?"

"It's up to her to explain," said Mr Gupta. "I'm certain it's all some terrible mistake."

He hurried away on his walking frame.

Gran wasn't in her room. I finally found her alone in the greenhouse, watering the tomato plants.

"Oh, Violet," she said. "It's terrible. They searched our rooms."

"Who searched your rooms?"

"The nurses." A tear rolled down Gran's face. I'd only ever seen her cry once before. (But they were tears of laughter when Dad was chased by an angry goose.)

"What's the matter?" I asked. "Riley said

something about people calling you a thief! But Mr Gupta says he doesn't believe a word of it. He says to tell you he's still your friend."

"He's a kind man." Gran wiped her eyes and turned back to the tomato plants.

"But they found it!" she said. "I don't know what to do."

"Found what?" I tried to get her to look at me but she wouldn't turn round.

"Mrs Paterson's diamond ring," she said. "It went missing. And they just found it. Hidden in my room!"

CHAPTER 11

Bridget, the pretty red-haired nurse at Sunset, helped me tuck Gran into bed for an early night.

"Don't you go worrying yourself now, Mrs Short," she said in her kind, rolling voice. "We'll get to the bottom of why that stolen ring was in your room, I'm sure of it."

But Gran knew that the retirement centre was full of whispers. She curled herself into a ball and closed her eyes. There was no point asking her anything about our shrinking secret tonight. I could see she was far too upset about being accused of stealing to think of anything else.

"Best let her rest," whispered Nurse Bridget.

"But why would anyone think Gran stole the ring?" I asked as we tiptoed down the hall. "Surely it got in her room by mistake?"

"There's a lot of valuable things been going missing," said Nurse Bridget. "Especially on the days when your grandma does Plant Patrol."

"Plant Patrol? What's that?"

"The old folks take it turns to do jobs for one another," Nurse Bridget explained. "Like going out to the postbox or picking up things from the chemist. Your gran's on Plant Patrol this month. That means she pops into everyone's rooms to water their pot plants and flowers."

"She does love plants," I said.

"Then the Collins sisters lost a pair of pearl earrings each," said Nurse Bridget.

I gasped. The old Collins twins, Cora and Dora, are two of Gran's closest friends. They all go to the theatre together – they're CRAZY about musicals and sit in the front row singing along at the top of their voices.

"And Mr Gupta lost his gold watch," said Nurse Bridget. "All on the days when your grandma was watering their plants. Of course, no one really believed she was the thief... Not until we searched the retirement centre and Mrs Paterson's ring was found in your grandma's room."

"But Mrs Paterson could have dropped the ring," I said. I remembered how she'd come into Gran's room with Riley. "She was in there last weekend. To fetch Barry Bling."

"Mrs Paterson never wears the ring. The diamonds are too precious. She keeps it locked away in her room," said Nurse Bridget. She laid her hand on my shoulder. "That's part of the problem, I'm afraid. The key to her drawer was hidden under the plant your grandma waters."

"But Gran would never steal anything!" I cried. Surely Nurse Bridget didn't really believe Gran was guilty.

"I'm sure she wouldn't." Nurse Bridget shook her head. "But the ring was found hidden in a mug, on your grandma's dressing table, right in front of her mirror."

My breath caught in my throat. "Her **WORLD'S BEST GRANNY** mug? I gave her that." The handle smashed when I was bouncing on Gran's bed one day. She refused to throw the mug away. She couldn't drink out of it any more, but she kept all her little trinkets and treasures inside.

"That's exactly where she would keep a ring," I gasped.

"Don't look so worried now." Nurse Bridget ruffled my hair. "I'm sure your grandma didn't take it. Just as soon as she's had a bit of rest, I'm sure she'll explain."

"I hope so," I said. "I just *know* she wouldn't have done this."

"I wish I could turn invisible," smiled Nurse Bridget. "I'd creep about and listen at keyholes. That way, I'd find out what was really going on!"

"INVISIBLE! OF COURSE! YOU'RE BRILLIANT!" " I threw my arms round Nurse Bridget's plump waist.

"Now what's got into you?" she laughed.

"Nothing," I shrugged. But a tiny little plan had started to form in my mind. I couldn't turn invisible, like Nurse Bridget had suggested. But if I could make myself shrink, I might just manage the next best thing!

CHAPTER 12

I was up early next morning.

"Poor Gran," said Mum, nibbling nervously on a slice of grapefruit. It's what she always eats for breakfast. Milky cereal disagrees with her. "The nurses say if they haven't found the thief by the end of the weekend, they might have to call the police in."

"THE POLICE!" I froze. "They can't do that! Will they arrest Gran? Will they throw her into prison like Ratty-Riley said they would?"

"Of course not. Don't be so dramatic, Violet," said Mum. "But—"

"It's Sunday today! That means the police will be coming tomorrow!" I rummaged frantically through the kitchen cupboards. "That only gives us one day to prove that Gran is innocent!"

The nurses would never be able to find out anything, unless they were lucky enough to stumble across the real thief and catch him or her red-handed. Nurse Bridget had said so herself – she said she'd need to be invisible. What Gran **REALLY** needed was a little help from someone like me! Someone tiny who could hunt for evidence without being seen.

There *had* to be some simple reason why the ring ended up in Gran's room.

"I'm going to go in and see Nurse Bridget as soon as she's finished her morning shift," said Mum. "We'll have a meeting and . . . Violet? What *are* you doing?"

I pulled six packs of wholemeal lentils and three bags of butter beans out of the cupboard and on to the table.

"Do we have any of that new Oaty Flake cereal left?" I said, searching through a shelf of rice cakes and herbal tea. "I had it for the first time the other day. When we went to the theme park."

MY PLAN WAS BRILLIANT AND SIMPLE!

If I could eat the same breakfast that I'd eaten on the morning I shrank in the PLUNGER! queue, then perhaps I'd shrink again today.

"But you said you didn't like Oaty Flakes,"

Mum frowned. "You said they tasted like hamster food . . . Dad and Tiff agreed."

She rummaged in a shopping bag behind the door.

"But I do have a surprise for you!" She held up a packet of cereal. "Ta-da! I brought you some

CHOCCY-CHIMPS!"

"Wow! For *me*?" I couldn't have been more surprised if

Mum had said I should become a vampire and drink a pint of fresh blood every morning. "*You* bought a packet of *chocolate* cereal for *me*?"

"Yes," Mum smiled. "I know how upset you were about that whole business with Lunger. . ."

"PLUNGER!"

"Right . . . and now you're worried about Gran. I thought a nice, naughty treat would cheer you up."

"Thanks, Mum!" I poured myself a bowl and watched as the milk turned chocolatey. Normally, I'd have been in junk-food heaven, but today each cheerful CHOCCY-CHIMP stuck in my throat – if only I could have had a bowl of *boring* Oaty Flakes instead. They were the secret to my shrinking – I was sure of it!

"If we didn't finish the Oaty Flakes," I said, as Mum headed out of the door for a shower, "where did the rest of them go?"

I knew Mum would never throw away good, healthy food.

"You know I don't eat cereal," said Mum, "and you all said they tasted like hamster food. So I fed them to Hannibal!"

She pointed to our hamster's cage and hurried away upstairs.

"**NO!**" My best chance of shrinking had been fed to our pet!

CHAPTER 13

I couldn't believe Mum had fed the rest of the Oaty Flakes to our hamster. Without eating them, I was sure I wouldn't be able to shrink. And if I couldn't shrink, I wouldn't be able to snoop secretly round the retirement centre, track down the real thief and prove it wasn't Gran who stole the ring.

I couldn't just nip out and buy a new pack either. Our local shop only sells delicious, sugary kinds of breakfast cereals. The kind that everyone – except Mum – wants to pop out and buy. To get more Oaty Flakes, I'd have to go all the way to the health food shop on the other side of town. There was no one to give me a lift just now. Dad had been called into work because of an emergency computer meltdown or something and Mum was still in the shower, getting ready for her meeting with Nurse Bridget.

I poured myself another bowl of **CHOCCY-CHIMPS** – OK, they didn't taste as good as normal ... but the MIRACLE of Mum actually letting me eat junk food was too good an opportunity to miss.

Why couldn't **CHOCCY-CHIMPS** be the secret to my shrinking? A little cocoa powder, a lot of sugar – **YUM!** Instead, I was supposed to act like a hamster and eat healthy Oaty... Wait a minute!

I leapt up, spilling my **CHOCCY-CHIMPS** across

the table. Mum said she'd fed the Oaty Flakes to Hannibal, but perhaps he hadn't eaten them all. He can be a very slow eater . . . always stuffing his cheeks.

I ignored the pool of chocolatey milk dripping off the table and peered into the hamster cage on the counter beside me.

"Hello, little fellow!"

Hannibal looked up, his cheeks stuffed full as if he knew I might be after the last of his dinner.

"It's all right," I whispered. "I just want to see if you've got any Oaty Flakes left."

I opened the cage and stretched my hand inside.

"YES!" Hannibal's bowl was nearly half full. "THIS IS GOING TO WORK!" I cried. "THIS IS TOTALLY, TOTALLY GOING TO

WORK!" My heart was beating like a tambourine at a school concert. I popped a handful of the flakes into my mouth.

I swallowed hard, forcing the dry cardboardy shavings down my throat. "And a few more to keep me going," I said, stuffing my dressing-gown pocket.

Everything was perfectly perfect at last! Now I'd eaten the Oaty Flakes, all I had to do was persuade Mum to take me with her when she went to see Nurse Bridget this morning. It had taken at least two hours between eating the breakfast cereal and starting to shrink in the PLUNGER! queue. So I'd have plenty of time now. I should be safely at the retirement centre long before I started to shrink!

I'd wait for Mum to finish her shower. Then I could go and see Gran, tell her my plan. I'd begin to investigate the moment I shrank.

I clapped my hands. Excitement B<small>UZ</small>ZED through me as I leant up on to the counter, jiggling my feet above the ground.

"I'm going to catch the thief!" I told Hannibal. I stretched my hand into the back of the cage to stroke him. "This is DEFINITELY, DEFINITELY going to wor... Whoa!"

My toes tingled. A strange flying sensation shot through my body, like I'd been pinged through the air on an elastic band.

"WHEE<small>EEEEEE!</small>"

I was plunging forward – tumbling head first into Hannibal's cage. I saw the kitchen roll and the kettle whooshing past – suddenly as big as giant skyscrapers on the counter beside me.

"Stop! Wait! I'm not supposed to be shrinking yet!"

The sawdust on Hannibal's floor seemed to be rushing up towards me. I threw my arms out to steady my fall. Beside me, on the bottom of the cage, was a sunflower seed. It was the same size as my tiny outstretched hand.

I rolled myself into a tight ball, tumbling forward until I came to a stop underneath Hannibal's water drinker.

"Wow!" I said. "The Oaty Flakes really worked!"

I jumped to my feet and stared up into the surprised eyes of my pet hamster. Hannibal was standing up on his hind legs, food popping out of the corner of his mouth. I've always thought of him as cute and cuddly ... but now he seemed more like a grizzly bear. Raised up on his legs, he was taller than me . . . and a lot fatter!

"T-t-thanks for letting me drop in like this!" I stuttered.

But Hannibal backed away. He seemed even more scared of me than I was of him.

"Don't worry. It's me! Violet!" I said. "I've shrunk, that's all!"

CHAPTER 14

Ten minutes later, I was pacing up and down the hamster cage. I rattled the bars, desperately trying to push open the door, which had swung closed behind me when I fell in. Hannibal seemed to have got used to the idea of a tiny girl. He only glanced up at me every once in a while now, between mouthfuls of food. I think he was trying to eat the last of the Oaty Flakes before I could.

"It's all right for you," I said. "You're used to being locked in here!"

I had no idea I was going to shrink so fast – right after eating the Oaty Flakes! Now, here I was, trapped inside the cage.

Gran was miles away on the other side of town and Mum would be leaving any minute to visit her.

I tried pushing the door again.

But I was too small and weedy to open the cage. If I could just get up a bit of speed . . . a bit of force . . . perhaps I could whack it open with some kind of cool, mini kung fu karate kick. (I knew I should have gone to kick-boxing classes at the Martial Arts School last summer instead of the Kids' Yoga Camp Mum sent me on.) Still, I'd have to try my best!

"HI YA!" I leapt over Hannibal and jumped on to his hamster wheel. If I could just get it spinning fast enough, I could leap off and fly through the air.

It's not as easy as it looks being a hamster! You have to run really, really fast to get the wheel spinning at all. But once you do get it going, it's an **AMAZING** feeling – better than being on the big wheel at the fair!

Hannibal must have thought it looked pretty fun too because he hopped on and joined me.

"Come on! Faster!" I urged as we both sped round together, the red plastic wheel spinning beneath us. Whoops! We must have gone a bit *too* fast.

I spun right up to the top of the wheel.

My feet

slipped.

I plunged

downwards
...

"Sorry!" I yelped as I landed SPLAT on Hannibal's back. My legs were either side of his chubby body as if I were riding a Shetland pony.

I thought I might have hurt Hannibal. But he jumped happily off the wheel with me clinging on like a jockey. He charged around the cage, leaping over half-chewed toilet rolls as if he were a race horse.

As we leapt up, I spotted that Mum and Tiffany had both come downstairs.

"HELLO!" I shouted. "OPEN THE CAGE!"

"What's the matter with that hamster, Tiff?" Mum's voice boomed from far away across the room. "Did you hear that funny squeaking sound?"

"Mum!" I cried. If she was out of the shower, she must be ready to go and see Gran. . .

I pulled myself up to get a better view. Stretching my arms out like a circus rider, I balanced shakily on Hannibal's back.

Mum was by the fridge. She was checking her watch.

"It wasn't Hannibal squeaking!" I called out. "It was me!"

"There he goes again," said Mum, grabbing her car keys. "He doesn't normally do that, does he?"

"Dunno?" shrugged Tiffany. She's not exactly Doctor Dolittle, the animal lover. Tiff's idea of keeping a pet is looking after her own hair.

Mum came over and peered down through the bars.

"MUM! Look! It's...!"

BAM!

Hannibal chose that exact moment to go *through* a toilet roll instead of *over* it.

I was toppled to the ground like a mini bowling pin.

OUFF! I lay on my back in the sawdust, the breath knocked out of me.

"He must be hiding somewhere," sighed Mum. "I've got to rush. Keep an eye on him, will you, Tiff?" She pulled on her coat. "And look after Violet, too. I think she's upstairs. She wanted to come but she's not even dressed and I can't be late for my meeting with Nurse Bridget."

"Oops!" Mum was right. I was still wearing my pyjamas and dressing gown. They were tiny now, of course . . . and I was so small, nobody would see me anyway!

"That's *so* unfair. Why do I *always* have to look after Violet?" moaned Tiffany.

But I didn't listen to another word.

Mum was heading for the Sunset Retirement

Centre! I needed to go with her if I was going to help Gran.

Her handbag was hanging on the back of the chair right below me...

If I could just kick the cage door open and land in the bag, I'd be on my way.

"Here goes!" I leapt back on to the wheel.

Hannibal jumped up too – a blur of toffee-coloured fur galloping in front of me as we spun.

"HI YA!" I cried as I leapt off the wheel. I flew through the air, my tiny foot ready to kick the cage door wide open.

CHAPTER 15

Everything went perfectly to plan . . . or *almost*.

WHAM! The cage door burst open!

"Cabin crew, ready for landing!" I cried. My feet skimmed the edge of the counter as I flew through the air and plopped safely into Mum's handbag.

What I hadn't expected was that Hannibal would follow.

"Eeeek!" He let out a strange, startled squeak as he jumped out of the cage and flew through the air after me.

FLUMP!

. . .He landed on my head.

"Ouch! Careful!" It's no joke, when you're tiny, having a hefty hamster fall on you like a podgy Kung-Fu Panda.

"Time you cut down on those Oaty Flakes!" I warned him as he rolled sideways and nibbled on the corner of Mum's purse.

"See you later, Tiffany!" said Mum as she

grabbed her handbag and swung it on to her shoulder.

WHUMP! Hannibal and I crashed into each other again.

"See you later, Violet!" Mum called. I managed to scramble upright and caught sight of the banisters through the top of the open bag as she hurried out of the hall.

I heard Mum slam the front door and the sound of her shoes crunching across the gravel on the driveway. Her key beeped as she opened the car and tossed her bag inside.

"Geff off!" I mumbled through a mouthful of fur as Hannibal sat on my head yet again.

Mum always drives really S - L - O - W - L - Y and really C - A - R - E - F - U - L - L - Y.

(I think it's all that lettuce she eats – it makes her drive like a snail!)

But she must have been worried about Gran, or scared she'd be late for her meeting with Nurse Bridget, because she bounced over some of the speed bumps – sending me and Hannibal rattling around again. And she revved her engine – almost deafening us – whenever she was stopped at the traffic lights. She even honked her horn at one driver and said a really rude word *!*!*!*! (which she *definitely* wouldn't have said if she'd known I was hiding in her handbag).

I nearly jumped up and told her to pay a pound to our family swear box. At least if she saw how tiny I was, she'd have to believe I'd told the truth about shrinking at the theme park. But I stopped myself.

"If Mum saw me now, she'd get such a shock she'd crash the car!" I told Hannibal. Of course, he couldn't understand a word I said. He carried on shredding a pack of tissues so that he could make a bed in the bottom of Mum's bag.

I scratched him behind the ear (which, now I was tiny, was more like petting a pony than a hamster).

"The last thing we need is Mum in a panic," I said.

Mum is so determined that me and Tiff will grow up big and strong, she makes us eat *nine* portions of fruit and veg a day. If she saw that I really *had* shrunk to the size of a carrot stick, she'd speed straight to the hospital. She'd make the doctors keep me in a plastic bubble for the rest of my life! I'd have to live on nothing but healthy cabbage soup and mushed courgettes fed to me through a tube.

"And I'll be NO use to Gran in a plastic bubble!" I told Hannibal, as Mum stopped the car. "I have to prove she's innocent and discover everything I can about the jewellery thefts."

We'd reached the Sunset Retirement Centre at last. I peeped over the top of the handbag as Mum swung it over her shoulder and set off towards Gran's room.

"Just keep your head down and DON'T make a squeak, Hannibal!" I warned him as we hurried through the lounge.

Mum pushed open Gran's bedroom door and tiptoed inside.

"Hello, Ma! Are you awake?" she said softly.

When I peered out of the bag, I could see that Gran was either asleep or hiding under the covers.

It didn't look like she was going to say much again today.

"See you later, Hannibal," I whispered. He scratched his ear and looked at me blankly, but it made me feel better to talk to someone. "You stay here and eat the rest of the tissues. I'm going to creep down to the lounge and see what I can find out. With any luck, the REAL thief will be acting suspiciously. . ."

Hannibal stuffed another mouthful of tissue into his cheeks.

"Good! That's a plan then!" I said.

But as I looked down my head spun. Leaping from the handbag on Mum's shoulder would be like jumping from a ten-storey building.

I grabbed the only tissue Hannibal hadn't nibbled.

"Sorry, but I need that for a parachute."

I clambered up on to the edge of the handbag, holding the tissue out above my head.

My legs were shaking as I balanced on the zip. Far beneath me, the brown carpet spread out like a ploughed field below an aeroplane.

"Three . . . two . . . one. GO!"

I hesitated before I jumped, wondering if the plan would work. Would the tissue be strong enough to hold me? Would I fall to the ground like a stone? But then Mum took a step forward. I was thrown off the edge of the bag and – **WHOOSH!** – the tissue filled with air.

"Perfect!" I floated gently down to the floor like a feather. Ha! Now I'd been skydiving . . . and I didn't even have to wait for Dad to agree.

As soon as I hit the ground, I dodged Gran's
closing door and sped away down the corridor. A
jagged rip in the carpet sent me flying flat on to my
nose. But I picked myself up and kept close to the
wall.

ON and **ON** I ran. It felt like I was
running a marathon instead of making my way

down a corridor. I stopped for a moment, gasping for breath. As I looked up, the last person I expected to see was Ratty-Riley.

But there he was, coming along the corridor. I recognized his **BIG**, GREY, **SMELLY** trainers right away.

It's amazing what you can learn from someone's feet when you're down at the same level at their shoes. I noticed at once that there was something odd about the way Riley was moving. He wasn't running or walking down the corridor . . . he was *creeping*. That's the only word for it. His trainers weren't making any sound at all.

I spy with my <u>little</u> eye somebody up to no good! I thought.

As he tiptoed closer, I looked up at Riley's

face. He was chewing his bottom lip and glancing nervously back over his shoulder with every step he took.

"Nan?" he whispered, crouching down outside Mrs Paterson's door. "Nan? Are you in there?" He peered through the keyhole.

I was right beside Riley now, hoping he wouldn't look down... Apart from anything else, I was still wearing my tiny dressing gown and spotty cow-print pyjamas! And what if I were to suddenly grow tall again? How would I explain that?

"Nan?" he whispered again. There was no answer from Mrs Paterson's room. But Riley opened the door anyway and slunk inside *very* quietly.

Why was Riley acting so suspiciously? Why

was he going into his grandmother's room when he knew she wasn't there? This was the very same room where the diamond ring had been stolen. . .

Wait a mini moment! Could Riley Paterson be the thief?

One thing was certain. Whatever he was up to, I was going to follow him and find out!

CHAPTER 16

I dived into Mrs Paterson's room, rolling on to my hands and knees before the door slammed shut.

BANG!

Riley jumped guiltily at the sound. He didn't spot me crawling across the rug like a very big beetle (but a very small girl).

He headed straight for his grandma's bedside table and tried to open the top drawer. It must have been locked, though, because after he rattled it a few times he gave up and hurried over to the window sill.

"It *might* still be here..." he muttered to himself.

I edged across the carpet, hiding behind a pair of Mrs Paterson's slippers as I stood up on tiptoe to try to see what he was doing. He lifted the plant – the same one my gran had watered – and took a **shiny** gold key from underneath it.

So he *was* up to no good! That was the key to Mrs Paterson's jewellery drawer. I remembered it was hidden under her plant pot. That's why everyone thought Gran had found the key and stolen the diamond ring when she was on Plant Patrol.

I couldn't believe Mrs Paterson was still hiding the key in the same place.

"Got it!" grinned Riley.

But I was ahead of him! I sprinted across the rug (which was about the length of a football pitch to me now). Then I hauled myself up the cable of the bedside lamp as if I were climbing a rope. Thank goodness for the hours I've spent in the playground at King's Park. If you don't want to use the ladder to climb to the highest slide, you can get there by a rope instead, and I *never* use the ladder. Perfect practice for a tiny spy, it turns out!

I scrambled on to the bedside table and crouched down behind the lamp. Riley came back across the room with the key.

He was so excited about whatever it was he

was hoping to find, he began nibbling his nails and making funny little squeaking sounds.

Sometimes I really do think that boy is three quarters *actual proper* RAT!

"Eeee. Eeee. Tee-hee!" he squeaked, slipping the key into the lock.

This was it! My palms felt sweaty. I was gripping the lamp so hard, I left small damp fingerprints on the brass. I was in the PERFECT place to see everything . . . Riley was about to steal a piece of Mrs Paterson's jewellery. I was sure of it!

He jiggled the drawer open.

My heart was pOUNDING. Now I could prove it wasn't Gran who was the thief . . . it was Riley-the-Robber. A **TOTAL** rat who'd steal from his own grandma!

"Tee, eee, eee," squeaked Riley again, grinning from ear to ear. His hand shot into the drawer.

I saw a flash of **gold** as his fingers closed around something small and shiny inside.

Was it a ring? A necklace, maybe?

Riley slipped the treasure into his pocket and locked the drawer.

"Caught you!" I mouthed silently. I punched my tiny fist in the air. As soon as I grew tall again, I'd grab Riley by the collar and march him straight to Nurse Bridget. I'd prove *he* was the real thief.

"Whoops!" I was wriggling so much with excitement, I stumbled backwards and fell off the edge of the bedside table.

"Whoa!" I would have plunged to my death if I hadn't managed to grab hold of the edge of Mrs P's bedtime book as I fell.

"What was that?" said Riley. He spun round.
I stayed hidden d^angl^ing from the book down the
far side of the table. My fingers gripped the pages,
clinging on to them like rocks on a mountainside.

Riley turned
away again.
He put the
key back
under the
plant pot.
By the time I'd
scrambled back on to
the table, he was heading for the door. I
staggered to my feet. If Riley left the room
without me there was no way I'd be able to

reach the doorknob. I'd be locked in Mrs Paterson's room ... perhaps till I grew back to my normal size. That might be hours yet. I had no idea how long my shrinking would last.

I had to be quick; if I lost sight of Riley he might stash the stolen gold somewhere outside. Then I'd never be able to prove that he was the thief.

I looked around, desperately planning my quickest escape route. If I could roll off the other side of the table, the soft bed would catch me like a trampoline. Then I could slide down the duvet on to the floor and catch up with Riley near the door. If the worst came to the **VERY** worst I could jump on to his stinky trainers and hitch a ride. Just like I'd done with Dad at the theme park.

"Here goes!" I whispered under my breath.

I h u r l e d myself towards the bed. There was no time to waste. Except . . . what was he *doing*?

As he reached the middle of the room, Riley caught sight of himself in his grandma's big mirror.

"Hey there!" he said, clicking his fingers at his own reflection.

He stood posing in front of the wardrobe door as if he were having his picture taken in a photo booth.

I was only halfway across the bed, but I stopped and stared. Riley turned his head from side to side, trying out three or four different kinds of grin — each one more ratty than the last.

"Looking good!" he told his reflection.

This was too much! I thought my little stomach was going to burst from holding my laughter inside.

Riley posed again.

"Say cheese, Ratty-Riley," I giggled to myself. And then. . .

whOOSH!

"Oh no!" I knew this feeling.

I grabbed hold of the duvet and tried to hide under it. But it was hopeless. My head spun. My stomach lurched and . . . WHAM! . . . I'd grown back to my FULL SIZE.

"Help!" Riley leapt into the air. "What are you doing here?" he squealed. He was so surprised, he tripped over Mrs Paterson's slippers, toppled backwards and landed flat on his bum.

"Why are you in my grandma's bed?" he gasped. "And why are you wearing pyjamas. . .?"

CHAPTER 17

"Thief!" yelled Riley at the top of his lungs. "Thief! Come quick!"

Moments later it seemed as if all the residents of the Sunset Retirement Centre were crowded into Mrs Paterson's bedroom. And they were **ALL** staring at me!

"Violet was sneaking about in here!" said Riley. He popped something into his mouth and chewed on it like a rat with a chunk of cheese. "I bet she's the one who stole the jewels!"

"Me? But—"

"This is too much for my poor weak heart," cried Mrs Paterson. "I should have known the girl was a thief! Just like her grandmother! A rotten apple never falls far from the tree!"

"*And* she's got dreadful nits!" said Barry Bling, as if this had something to do with it. "She's absolutely infested!"

Everyone took a step backwards.

"Now hold on," said Mr Gupta kindly. "I'm sure Violet can explain."

"Yes, I can!" I stared hard at Barry Bling. "I *haven't* got nits! I *haven't* stolen anything. And I *wasn't* doing anything wrong."

But just at that moment, Mum appeared in the doorway. "Violet?" she said, pushing her way through the crowd. "What are you doing here? I thought you were at home!" Her face flushed as red as the tomato soup she'd made us eat last night. "How did you get here? And *why* are you wearing pyjamas?"

"I think you'd better try to explain yourself," said Nurse Bridget. For the first time since I'd known her, she didn't look kind and friendly. She was staring at me with her hands on her hips.

"I – er – I wanted to visit Gran," I said. "I came into Mrs Paterson's room because . . . because. . ."

Something told me this wasn't the moment to tell everyone how I'd shrunk to the size of a door key, got stuck in a hamster cage and travelled here in a handbag! The old folks were already staring at me as if I were MAD, **BAD** and DANGEROUS.

Plus, they'd all moved away from me,

132

scratching their heads, since Barry had mentioned the nits.

"I saw Riley acting suspiciously," I said. "So I followed him in here to find out what he was up to."

"Good thinking," nodded Cora – one of the Collins twins, who are best friends with Gran. Mum can never tell them apart. But it's easy. Cora's the one who has freckles on her nose – like me. Dora is the one who doesn't.

"I saw Riley take a key from under the plant," I said.

"That's the key Mrs Paterson uses to lock away her jewellery!" gasped Dora.

"Exactly!" I said. "And Riley unlocked Mrs Paterson's drawer and took something out of it.

He's the jewellery thief! I'm sure of it."

Now everyone was staring at Riley as if *he* was

MAD, **BAD** and DANGEROUS.

"What?" All the colour drained from Riley's

face. He was chewing harder than ever.

"You're a stinky rotten liar, Violet Potts!" he mumbled.

"What's that in your mouth, then?" I said. "I bet you're trying to swallow the evidence!"

But I was a moment too late. Riley gulped and opened his mouth to show it was empty.

"I never stole any jewellery!" he said. "I was just minding my *own* business in my *own* grandmother's room! Violet's the one who broke in here!" He stuck out his tongue. "She's just trying to turn the blame on me."

"That's right!" said Mrs Paterson. "It's obvious what's happened! Violet must have crept in here to steal the rest of my jewellery! Her grandmother took my diamond ring and Violet came back to **finish the job**."

"An *accomplice*!" tutted Barry Bling.

"Honestly!" said Mum. "I think that's going a bit far!"

"Never trust children," said Barry, running his

fingers through his long golden curls. "Never trust them! That's all I can say!"

"Your grandmother's always admired my precious antique locket. It's Victorian," said Mrs Paterson, poking her finger at me. "Is that why you came in here? To steal my locket?"

" **NO!** " I'd seen Riley take something shiny from the drawer. I had to prove he was the thief, otherwise everyone would go on believing that me and Gran had formed some sort of terrible robber gang.

"Is the locket gold, Mrs Paterson?" I asked. "About the size of a ten-pence piece?"

"Ha!" cried Riley. "How would Violet know that unless she was the thief?"

"Good point!" said Barry Bling.

"I know because I saw *you* pinch something **gold** and sparkly, Riley!" I said. "I was *hiding* all the time." (No need to mention I was actually so small I was on the bedside table, crouched behind the lamp.) "I saw everything you did."

"She's a liar!" mumbled Riley, but I noticed his hand shot down the side of his leg. He was fiddling with his tracksuit bottoms. Perhaps he hadn't swallowed the evidence after all!

"Ask him to empty his pockets right now," I said, turning to Nurse Bridget. "Then we'll soon see who's a liar!"

Riley tried to protest. But there was nothing for it.

"It's the only honourable thing to do!" said Mr Gupta.

"Fine!" said Riley. But his hands were shaking as he dug into his pockets.

I almost felt sorry for him. But at least now I could prove Gran was innocent.

"See!" said Riley. "Nothing there!" He emptied a dirty tissue, a broken biro and a plastic pirate toy on to the bed.

"Wait a minute!" I was too quick for him. I'd seen a tiny shimmer of gold. "Look under the tissue!" I cried. "He's trying to hide something!"

Normally nothing in the ENTIRE WORLD would have persuaded me to go anywhere near Riley's snotty hankie. But now I grabbed the broken biro and flicked the tissue out of the way to show everyone what was underneath.

"See!" I crowed. **"Gold!"**

The old folks pushed past me and crowded round the bed.

"Well, I suppose it *is* gold, dear," said Cora. "But. . ."

"But what?" I cried. "How much more proof do you need?"

"A little more than that, I'm afraid!" said Nurse Bridget, making room so that I could see the bed.

"It *is* gold," said Dora. "Except . . ."

" . . . it's only a chocolate wrapper!" I groaned. The shimmering jewel I'd seen was nothing more than a shiny ball of gold foil.

Riley was looking at his feet.

"Sorry, Nan," he blushed. "I did unlock the drawer . . . and I took one of your chocolates."

A chocolate! Great! And I'd accused Riley of

being a top-class jewellery thief!

"As long as it wasn't a toffee one you took!" said Mrs Paterson.

"Er..." Riley blushed more than ever. He really did look sorry.

"I didn't used to be able to enjoy toffees," Mrs Paterson told Mum. "But I've just discovered this new glue for my false teeth. **FIXAGUM!** It holds the teeth in place perfectly, even with the stickiest, chewiest toffee..."

Of course! A sticky toffee! That was what Riley had been chewing so hard.

"**FIXAGUM** is brilliant!" grinned Barry Bling. "I mean ... er ... I've heard it's really strong." He shot us all a perfect white smile, as if to prove that his own teeth were real.

"You're a naughty boy, Riley!" sighed Mrs Paterson.

"Naughty," agreed Mr Gupta. "But not a criminal! I myself have a very sweet tooth."

He ruffled Riley's hair and handed him a mint humbug. (One of the mint humbugs he would normally give to *me*!)

"Riley's certainly not a jewellery thief!" nodded Cora.

"Still doesn't explain what Violet was doing here," said Barry.

"I've told you. I followed Riley," I said. "I was... Well, I was running along the corridor ... and he seemed to be acting strangely."

"I never saw you!" said Riley.

"That's because you were too busy **creeping**

about," I said.

I dug into my dressing-gown pockets.

"I didn't steal anything. Look! Nothing but Oaty Flake cereal," I said, opening my hand.

"There isn't anything else in there," agreed Cora.

"It does look like she's telling the truth," said Dora.

"Thank you!" I smiled at the twins.

"I still don't understand why she's wearing pyjamas," said Barry, shaking his head.

"What you choose to wear isn't a crime, though. Is it, dear?" whispered Cora, putting her arm around me.

"Certainly not," giggled Dora. "Otherwise Barry would be arrested for that purple shirt!"

"My poor heart," said Mrs Paterson, clutching

the window sill. "This has all been too much for me."

"I'm sorry. I shouldn't have come into your room," I said. "I was just trying to help and—"

"Don't let me catch you snooping about in here again," she sniffed. "Especially when my grandson is minding his own business!"

She unlocked the drawer and held up her gold locket.

"See. Everything is where it's supposed to be."

"Perhaps we should have done that in the first place," sighed Nurse Bridget.

"And perhaps Violet should have checked her facts!" snapped Mrs Paterson.

OK. I suppose I *might* have jumped to a couple of tiny wrong conclusions.

"Everyone knows your grandma is the *real* thief!" said Riley. "How else did that diamond ring end up in her room?"

CHAPTER 18

"I can't believe it, Violet!" Mum bustled me into Gran's room and shut the door. "All you've managed to do is make everything worse!" Her face was still as red as tomato soup. But she was so furious, **steam** was practically coming out of her ears!

"I thought you were at home. How did you even manage to get here?" she whispered, trying not to wake Gran, who still seemed to be asleep under the covers. "And *why* are you wearing pyjamas?"

"It's a long story," I said, keeping my voice down too.

I glanced over at the lump in the bed. I didn't really believe Gran was asleep. Normally, she'd be at her ballroom dancing class, helping in the garden, or playing bingo in the lounge. I'd never seen her stay in bed all day. Ever! She must be hiding away here, too ashamed to show her face. She was sure all her friends thought she was the thief.

I had to do *something*. It was time to try and make Mum believe the truth. If I could convince her, we might find a way to clear Gran's name.

"I came here in your handbag," I whispered.

"*In* my *handbag*?" Mum's eyes were as wide as rice cakes.

"Yes. That's why I'm still wearing my pyjamas," I said. "I jumped in your bag before you left home. It happened again, Mum. I shrun—"

"Oh no! Don't you start that!" Mum wasn't even trying to whisper now. "I don't want any more of that shrinking nonsense, Violet!"

Gran sat bolt upright in bed. Her hair was sticking up in all directions like a scarecrow.

"Shrinking?" she said. "Of course!"

I ran over to the bed and grabbed Gran's hand. Mum would have to believe me if Gran told her the shrinking was true.

"I knew I could make it happen again," I said. "I ate some Oaty Flakes and next thing I knew . . . WHOOSH! I was tiny."

I explained how I'd escaped from Hannibal's

cage and hitched a ride to the retirement centre.

"I even heard Mum swearing in the car," I said. "She told one driver he was a—"

"Thank you, Violet! That's quite enough." Mum was as purple as an angry beetroot now. "What did Dad and I say about telling lies?"

I looked at Gran, begging her to help me. But she was lying back on her pillow again, lost in thought.

"Wait!" I could prove I was telling the truth! Hannibal was still in Mum's handbag. "I want to show you something," I said. "Have a look in your. . ."

But just at that moment, Mum's mobile phone rang.

"That must be Tiffany wondering where

you've got to." Mum scrabbled about in her bag. "Hello? Tiff? Hello? **Ahhhhhhhhhhhhhhhhhh!**" Mum screamed.

She'd grabbed hold of Hannibal and was holding him to her ear, shouting into his fluffy belly button as if he were her mobile phone.

She must have squeezed him too tight, though, because Hannibal wriggled round and bit her thumb.

"**Ouch!**" Mum let him go. Hannibal jumped out of her hand and shot under Gran's bed.

"I tried to warn you he was in there," I said.

"I suppose you put him there to trick me?" sighed Mum. She tried to wrap a bit of tissue round her thumb. But Hannibal had chewed all the tissues to shreds.

"I've got quite enough to worry about, Violet, without you playing silly games, wearing pyjamas and pretending to shrink," said Mum.

"I'm not preten—"

"You'd better catch Hannibal quick, or he'll disappear under the floorboards," said Mum in her <u>NO</u>-nonsense voice. "Look after Gran. I'm going to go and get a plaster from the first-aid room. Then I'll try and call Tiffany ... on my *proper* mobile phone!"

"But..."

"I need to get back to my important meeting with Nurse Bridget – which you interrupted with all that commotion."

That was so unfair. I was only trying to help.

Before I could say another word, Mum swept out of the room.

Perhaps she was right. I *had* made everything worse. And now I'd lost our hamster too!

"Hannibal?" I called as I crouched down to look for him. But Gran jumped out of bed so fast she almost landed on my head.

"Shrinking!" she said, grabbing my hands and spinning me round the room as if we were at some CRAZY ballroom dancing class. "It's wonderful, Violet! Don't you see? Your shrinking will put everything right!"

Chapter 19

Gran had **EXACTLY** the same idea as me.

"As soon as you can shrink, you'll be my inch-high spy!" she grinned. "Together we'll prove I am innocent!"

Our plan was simple. Gran knew the retirement centre inside out. She could drop me off in the offices, the kitchen or the dayroom. Anywhere we wanted to go. I'd listen in on every whispered conversation ... snoop into every tiny nook and cranny.

"If I eat these it won't take long," I said. "I'll

shrink to the perfect, pocket-sized detective!" I dug

into my dressing gown and stuffed a handful of Oaty

Flakes into my mouth. Then I sprinkled a couple of

crumbs on the floor and peered under the bed.

"Hannibal!" I called, trying to tempt him out.

But there was no sign of him.

"If only Mum had believed I shrunk, he

probably wouldn't even be under there," I sighed.

"I'm afraid people never do believe you."

Gran shook her head. "Family can be the worst.

My poor old mother refused to *ever* admit I was a

shrinker . . . even after she found me on top of the

Christmas tree one year. She just carried on as if

everything was normal."

"At least I've got you," I smiled as I stuffed

another couple of Oaty Flakes into my mouth.

"You'll *always* believe me!"

There were a million questions I wanted to ask Gran. Like, how long the shrinking would last? Or how often could it happen? Did it always happen in the daytime? Or sometimes at night? And I was desperate to hear about all the scrapes and adventures she'd had as a tiny girl. But there was no time for that now. I had to get on and shrink so that we could explore before Mum finished her meeting with Nurse Bridget and came to take me home.

I popped another dry, dusty flake into my mouth and chewed.

"What are you eating that horrible stuff for?" asked Gran. "It's not your mum's latest health snack, is it?"

"I told you. Oaty Flakes are the secret, mystery

ingredient that make me shrink," I said. "I'm sure of it."

"Really?" said Gran. "I never. . ."

"They worked the morning I went to the theme park. And they worked in Hannibal's hamster cage too," I said, popping three more flakes into my mouth.

"Here! Try one!"

I offered Gran a flake. She puffed out her cheeks like a hamster.

"Chomp! Chomp!" she grinned.

It was wonderful to see her almost back to her old happy self. If our **BRILLIANT** shrinking plan worked, she'd soon be ready to face her friends – no longer embarrassed that they thought she was a thief.

"I know it's silly," she said, frowning again. "I just feel no one really believes the ring got into my room by mistake. If we can find the true thief, we'll prove once and for all that I have nothing to hide."

I watched as she chewed the flake I'd given her, wrinkling her nose like a hamster.

"Gran?" I gasped. "You can't still shrink, can you?" Why hadn't I thought of it earlier? It would be BRILLIANT! We could snoop around together.

But Gran shook her head.

"I haven't been able to do that for years, dear," she said. "Not since I was a girl."

It was hard to imagine Gran as a little girl ... let alone a REALLY little girl the size of one of the pink wafer biscuits she loves so much.

"And it was never cereal that made me shrink anyway," she said.

"What was it, then?" I asked, picking up a glass of water from her bedside table and taking a gulp to wash down another mouthful of flakes. "Tell me it wasn't Brussels sprouts? That would be AWFUL."

"No!" laughed Gran.

"Pink biscuits?"

"No! I've been trying to tell you. With me, it wasn't anything like that," said Gran. "It wasn't things I ate. All it took to make me shrink was a bit of excitement!"

"Excitement? What do you mean?"

"Exactly that," said Gran. "Whenever I got *really* excited about anything ... WHOOSH! ... I'd shrink on the spot!"

"Wow!" I spat a mouthful of Oaty Flakes into the bin. What Gran was saying sent a tingle down my spine. "It was being excited that made you shrink?"

"Easy as that!" smiled Gran. "Of course, I used to shrink all the time! I was a *very* excitable child."

"Me too!" I grinned.

I remembered how **VERY** excited I'd been

right before I shrank the first time.

"I was SUPER-DUPER

WORLD-RECORD-BREAKING

excited," I told Gran. "I was about to ride PLUNGER!"

"And the next time?" asked Gran.

I thought for a moment.

"Yes! I was excited then too. I'd just seen the Oaty Flakes in Hannibal's cage . . . I really believed they'd make me shrink."

"That's it, then!" smiled Gran. "It works the same way. Every time you get overexcited . . . WHOOSH! . . . You'll shrink!"

"But I'm excited now!" I said, throwing the last handful of cereal into the bin. "I'm excited I don't have to eat any more Oaty Flakes for a start!"

"Yippee!" cried Gran.

"And I'm REALLY excited I know what makes me shrink!" I le^{apt} into the air and did a ⟨star⟩ jump to prove it.

"Then it might work right now," said Gran. "Are your toes tingling? Do you feel fuzzy? Light-headed?"

"A bit!"

Gran and I sped over to the mirror so that I could see for myself if anything would happen.

But nothing did.

"Come on! SHRINK!" I said, dancing a little jig. "I feel really **excited**. I really, really, really do!"

But deep down inside, my stomach felt strange and tight. Perhaps it was all the Oaty Flakes I'd eaten. Or perhaps it was that I knew we were running out of time. It was Monday morning tomorrow. If we didn't solve the crime, the police would come and. . .

I watched in the mirror as a wrinkly, crinkly frown crossed my face.

The knot in my stomach got tighter.

I felt the last tingle of excitement flicker like a candle flame inside me . . . and blow out.

"It's hopeless!" I said, flopping down on Gran's bed. "This is never going to work. I'm sorry!"

Chapter 20

While Mum was still in her meeting with Nurse Bridget, Gran and I tried everything to make me excited enough to shrink. Chocolate ice cream, dance music, jumping off the wardrobe... Nothing worked. Gran even promised to take me for a ride on PLUNGER! just as soon as we'd solved the jewellery crime.

But even that did no good. All I could think about was what would happen if the police were called tomorrow. My imagination was running wild, thinking of Gran locked up in chains like a prisoner in dungeon ... maybe with a fiery dragon guarding the cell.

"One thing's certain," said Gran. "If we can't prove I'm innocent, I won't stay at Sunset any more."

"But you love it here," I said.

Gran shook her head. "They'll probably throw me out. Even if they don't, I won't stay," she sighed. "Not with everyone whispering behind my back, thinking I might be a thief."

"I'm so sorry, Gran!" I said. "I was sure I'd be able to help you. I've let you down."

"Nonsense. It's not your fault, pet," said Gran. "But I think I'll have a little rest."

Although it was only twelve o'clock and a lovely bright day, she slipped back into bed and pulled the duvet over her head.

I knew Gran wasn't really tired. She was

hiding again.

"Great work, Violet!" I told myself as I drew the curtains and tiptoed out into the corridor. I *hadn't* managed to shrink . . . but I had managed to make Gran worried sick.

At the end of the corridor I saw the door out to the veranda – a long wooden deck which overlooks the yoga lawn. Just a week ago, Gran had been out there planting tubs of spring flowers – bossing Cora and Dora about and sending Mr Gupta for a watering can. How different everything was now. I sighed and headed down the corridor.

The veranda was a lovely spot. Perhaps if I went out there and sat in the sun, I might feel better. I might even feel EXCITED enough to shrink. Yes! I'd find a nice big chair, close my eyes and think about summer holidays. Or Christmas. Or my birthday. Or summer holidays, Christmas *and* my birthday all rolled into one. . .!

But as soon as I opened the big screen door, I regretted it.

Barry Bling was on the veranda. He was giving Mrs Paterson a face mask on one of the sun loungers.

"It's a good job you brought me out here, Barry," said Mrs Paterson. "I wouldn't want any of this gloop on the nice carpet in my room!" She pointed to the browny-green goo dripping off her chin.

"This isn't gloop!" cried Barry, smearing the mixture over her forehead. "This is finest River Nile mud all the way from Egypt!"

More likely soil from the bottom of the garden, I thought. I slipped into a tall sun chair before they noticed me.

It's hard to make yourself invisible when you're FULL SIZE, but I pulled my feet up underneath me and snuggled down into the enormous high-backed seat. I was facing away from Barry and Mrs Paterson and they were busy with their beauty treatment anyway.

No one could see me now, unless they walked round and stood right in front of the chair.

The seat was made from that plaited wicker stuff, like a basket. If I peered really carefully through the cracks in the weaving behind me, I could still see Barry and Mrs Paterson. But I tried to ignore them. I stared out at the yoga lawn, trying to think of exciting things.

There was nobody working in the gardens today, of course, because it was Sunday. Not that weekends seemed to keep Barry away. He was always here … giving beauty treatments … shouting about children having nits even when they **DON'T!**

"No!" I told myself. "Don't think about that!

You're supposed to be thinking about exciting things . . . and nits are <u>NOT</u> exciting!"

I had a vision of Mum attacking my hair with her fine-toothed, KILLER NIT COMB!

I shuddered and snapped out of my daydream in time to hear Barry and Mrs Paterson talking about Gran.

"There's no way she can deny it!" said Mrs Paterson. "My diamond ring was found hidden in that BEST GRANNY mug on her dresser."

"It's disgraceful!" said Barry.

I tucked my feet up higher and hugged my knees inside the chair. I tried not to listen to them.

Hearing bad things about Gran was *not* going to help me feel excited. At this rate I'd

NEVER shrink! The gnawing feeling in my stomach had started again – like a hamster nibbling in my belly. I wished I could get up and walk away. But that's the trouble with being full size. If I got out of the chair now, Barry and Mrs Paterson would see me.

"And that nosy granddaughter of hers is no better," said Mrs Paterson, as if she'd read my thoughts. "Did you see the way she picked on my poor little Riley?"

Poor little Riley? I had never heard anything so **TOTALLY RIDICULOUS** in my whole life! Mrs Paterson ought to see the way Riley picks on the smaller kids at school. Last week he poured water on the chalk pictures the nursery children had drawn in the playground. And he locked

Maisy Willis from reception in the ball cupboard for the whole of break.

I peered through the back of the chair. I couldn't see Mrs Paterson's eyes because Barry had covered them up with cucumber slices, but her wrinkly mouth was bent down in an angry frown. With her round cucumber eyes and muddy green face, she looked like a big cross frog. *Ribbit!*

"I don't trust that Violet Potts," she croaked. "Or her grandmother."

"Quite right," said Barry. "I hope you've moved your locket and put it somewhere really safe."

"Oh yes!" said Mrs Paterson. "It's in the safest place I could think of! I'm wearing it. See?" She pulled down the edge of her collar to show Barry the chain. I saw the glint of **GOLD** around her neck.

"Very sensible!" said Barry, patting the enormous diamond 𝔅-for-Barry on the thick gold chain around his own neck. "Wearing precious jewels is the very best way to keep them safe." He wriggled his fingers to show off his chunky gold rings. "But let's stop thinking about all these unpleasant things, Mrs P. You'll give yourself more . . . I mean, *some* wrinkles! And it's not good for your poor heart either. Try to relax. . . . *Imagine you're a cloud . . . a light, fluffy, carefree cloud.*"

Oh no! Barry must have the same meditation CD as Mum! He began to hum.

"You're a fluffy, carefree cloud," he whispered. "I'll give you a massage, Mrs P? That'll *really* help you relax."

I watched as Barry straightened the cucumber slices on Mrs Paterson's eyes. He stepped round the back of the sun lounger to massage her shoulders.

As he pressed down with one hand, Barry took hold of Mrs Paterson's gold chain with the other.

"Just relax," he whispered. "Remember, you're a fluffy cloud in the big blue sky!"

Barry glanced around the veranda. I froze. But he couldn't see me. Even though I was still FULL SIZE, I was *completely* hidden by the ENORMOUS chair.

Barely daring to breathe, I watched as Barry unclipped the gold chain from around Mrs Paterson's neck. All the time he kept talking to her, massaging her shoulders and telling her to relax. He was stealing Mrs Paterson's locket right before my eyes!

My legs trembled. I couldn't believe what I was seeing. Barry Bling was the jewellery thief. I had caught him red-handed!

It seemed so obvious now. Why I hadn't

thought of it before? Barry was always going in and out of everyone's rooms. He had plenty of opportunities to steal things... He was always telling people to relax, or sticking cucumber slices on their eyes. And Barry really did love sparkly jewellery! Just look at his own collection of rings and gold chains.

I've done it! I've proved Gran innocent, I thought, jiggling my legs as I hugged them tightly. *I'll just watch what Barry does with the locket, then I'll run and get Nurse Bridget. She'll call the police.*

A big grin spread across my face. I had found the thief all by myself ... and I hadn't even needed to shrink to do it.

It was hard to keep still. I wanted to *clap my hands* and WHOOP and **cheer**.

I watched, excitement racing through me, as Barry slipped the locket into his. . .

"Oh no!"

I felt a tingle in my toes and. . .

WHOOSH!

My stomach lurched.

The next thing I knew, I'd slipped down behind the cushion on the chair.

I had shrunk.

I was no bigger than the diamond B hanging around Barry Bling's neck.

"This is not the right moment!" I groaned. "I'm trying to catch a thief!"

But right now I wasn't even big enough to catch a tennis ball. . .

CHAPTER 21

Shrinking was NOT what I had had in mind! But there wasn't a moment to lose. Now I knew Barry was the thief, I had to get help. I had to tell someone.

"Stay there and relax," said Barry as soon as he'd slipped the locket off Mrs Paterson's neck. "I'll pop inside and check on Cora and Dora. They're under the hairdryers. Don't move those cucumber slices! I'll be back to take your face mask off in a while."

"Stop! Thief!" I cried. But, even if I could have

shouted loud enough, my voice was muffled by the cushion I'd slipped behind. I heaved myself up, pushing my way through bits of fluff, a penny the size of a pizza and a pistachio shell I could have worn like a hat.

As soon as I was free, I scrambled down the side of the chair, using the holes in the wicker like the rungs of a ladder for my tiny feet. But it was slow work. By the time I'd climbed to the floor, Barry was already through the heavy screen door that led inside. It banged shut behind him.

"Now what?" I might as well have been locked behind a steel wall for all the chance I had of catching up with him. I ran along a crack in the wooden floor, the sun loungers throwing dark grey shadows above my head.

The door from the veranda was about FIFTY times taller than me. It would probably weigh about the same as a lorry would if I were full size. There was **NO <u>way</u>** I'd ever be able to push it open.

I thought about shaking Mrs Paterson – maybe climbing on top of her and pinching her nose. But what if she really *did* have a weak heart? The sight of me jumping up and down like a tiny, crazy Mrs Pepperpot might just finish her off for good.

I'd already been called a thief . . . I didn't want to be called a murderer as well!

"This is SO unfair!" I kicked at the door . . . and stubbed my toe. "Ouch!" I'd forgotten I was only wearing my slippers. "When I want to shrink, I don't. And when I don't want to shrink, I do!"

I was pacing up and down, trying to think what to do next, when I heard a sharp SQUEAK below me. I looked down and saw a familiar nose poking up through a hole in the wooden planks of the veranda.

"Hannibal!" I cried. "How did you get down there?"

Last time I'd seen him, he'd disappeared under Gran's bed.

"Of course!" There must be a whole network of underground passages beneath the floorboards of the old building. Just right if you're a hamster ... or a TINY LITTLE GIRL.

"Wait!" I cried as Hannibal's nose disappeared again. If I could follow him under the floorboards, I could probably get right down under the house. I might be able to find an underground route to

Cora and Dora's room. Then I could hide under their bed and keep an eye on Barry.

But by the time I squeezed through the TINY hole in the plank, Hannibal had vanished.

Never mind, I thought. As long as I followed the veranda all the way along, I would end up underneath the twins' room. The two old sisters shared the big double room at the front of the building. I'd heard Mrs Paterson complain how unfair it was – *"They have a best view from there! Right out over the gardens"* – so at least I knew which way I was going.

But what if I grow back to full size? I thought suddenly. It could happen anytime, without warning, like it had in the litter bin or on Mrs Paterson's bed. Then I'd be WEDGED down here – like Winnie-the-Pooh in a rabbit hole! Squashed like the layer of peanut butter in a peanut butter roll...

"Better keep moving," I told myself. "No time to hang around."

I raced along under the wooden veranda. I thought it would be dark down here, but it was more like running through a forest. Like when Dad takes us on country hikes at the weekend.

Sunlight poured in through the cracks in the planks above, just like it does through tall tress on a woodland path.

Of course if this really were a hike, Dad would have had all his gadgets with him – like a compass, hand-held satnav and mobile phone. We could have just phoned Cora and Dora and told them what was going on. But that was no use to me now. Dad was miles away at his work disaster. Even if I did have a phone, I was so small I'd have to jump on the buttons to dial it.

I ran on until I reached a solid brick wall ahead of me under the planks. This must mean I was at the end of the building, right by Cora and Dora's room.

I turned away from the speckled forest

sunlight of the veranda and peered through a crack in the bricks into the DEEP, **DARK BLACKNESS** under the house.

There was nothing else for it. I needed to squeeze through there, then find a gap in the floorboards and crawl up into the room above. I had to find Barry and see what he was up to. I turned my body sideways and wriggled through the tiny crack and into the foundations of the house. At least if there were any creepy crawlies or giant spiders down here, it was too dark to see them.

I took a step forward and tripped over something long and narrow – probably an electricity cable running up into the house.

"ACHOO!" I sneezed as I landed in a pile of dust.

As I pulled myself up, something dashed past me in the gloom.

"Hannibal?" I called hopefully. "Is that you?" Whatever it was – a spider . . . a mouse . . . a *rat* – it sounded like a small horse galloping past.

My legs wobbled like JELLY. I could barely move I was shaking so hard. I couldn't see my own feet. And my nose was so full of dust I felt like a mini-vacuum cleaner! The sooner I was out of here, the better.

"See you upstairs," I called to what I hoped was Hannibal still scratching away in the corner. "I'm getting out of here!"

I stretched my hands out in front of me and took three brave steps towards a tiny glimmer of light ahead.

"Ouch!" My fingers touched something boiling hot. It must be a water pipe. There was a cold one beside it too. Both pipes led up to a faint circle of light where they ran into the room above. The gap looked as if it was just big enough for me to squeeze through.

I wrapped my knees around the cold water pipe and started to climb. The metal was freezing, damp and slippery – but really it was just like the fireman's pole at King's Park.

High above me, I heard a voice that I recognized.

"The police will have no choice but to arrest Mrs Short!" said Barry loudly. He was talking about Gran again. "After all, the ring was found hidden in her room."

"You're a HORRIBLE, HORRIBLE liar!" I mouthed to myself as I climbed.

"I refuse to believe it's true," said the voice of one of the twins above me. "She's such a lovely lady. I know she would never do anything like that."

"Thank you!" I knew how happy Gran would be to hear her friends still trusted her, no matter what people like Barry might say.

"She is as honest as apple pie," agreed Cora.

I've always liked the twins.

"She's nothing but a criminal!" said Barry, his lies echoing through the floorboards. "It's a serious crime to steal jewellery. . ."

"Yes, it is a serious crime!" I whispered. "And you're going to pay for it, Barry Bling!" I heaved myself up to the very top of the pipe. The circle of light from the bedroom shone down through the hole in floorboard above me. "Just as soon as I'm BIG enough I'm going to tell everyone that YOU are the thief!"

CHAPTER 22

I squeezed myself up through the hole beside the water pipe and hid behind Cora and Dora's wastepaper bin.

It was clear now why Barry had been shouting so loud. He'd wheeled two of those old lady space-helmet hairdryers in here. Cora and Dora were underneath with hot air blowing in their ears.

Another perfect trick for a thief, I thought. No one could hear anything under those hoods. Or turn their heads. Or see what was going on behind them.

"I'll give you more heat!" shouted Barry. "I'm afraid it's a bit blowy, but your hair will be dry in no time."

"Goodness! That *is* hot!" cried Cora, who was under the dryer nearest the door.

"At least it'll kill any nits, if there really are any about!" giggled Dora.

"Don't even mention those horrible little creatures!" Barry clutched his chest. He ducked round the back of the dryers and peered into the big round mirror on Cora and Dora's wall. "Head lice like clean hair best, you know!" he said, scratching the thick blond curls poking up from the gap in his shirt. "That's why I worry so much!"

"YUCK!" I remembered the first time I'd seen Barry scratch his chest like that. It was in Gran's room when he was leaning over her dressing table.

"Of course!" I gulped. That must be how Mrs Paterson's diamond ring had ended up in the **WORLD'S BEST GRANNY** mug.

It made **TOTAL** sense! I grabbed the edge of the skirting board to steady myself. Barry must have dropped the ring by mistake when he was peering into Gran's mirror, scratching like mad!

"I'll turn the temperature one spot higher, ladies?" he called as he poked his head round the front of the dryers again. "Don't worry if you fall asleep, I'll wake you up when you're done."

Now what was he up to? As I peered round the wastepaper bin, I could see him glancing over to the chest of drawers, where there were two little jewellery boxes. One had a D for Dora on the side. The other had C for Cora.

Barry touched the bulging pocket on his purple shiny shirt. *That must be where he stuffs the stolen jewellery,* I thought. *That's why the ring fell out when he leant forward to scratch his chest.*

If I could just sneak up into his pocket, I could see if he'd put Mrs Paterson's locket in there too. And I'd be ready if he took anything of Cora's or Dora's. I'd have to be quick, though, so he didn't see me run across the floor.

"Get set..." I whispered under my breath. "Go!"

I SHOT OUT from behind the wastepaper bin and across the rug. I was on the toe of Barry's black leather cowboy boot in about two seconds flat. If there were a mini Olympics, I'd win a gold medal for the two-hundred-centimetre sprint!

Now all I had to do was climb up to Barry's shirt pocket and check for jewellery. It was a long w^{ay} ^{up.} But I was getting good at this – and he was busy staring in the mirror, fluffing up his hair.

Barry's cowboy boots were a great help. They had blue shiny jewels spread out up the sides, like the footholds on a climbing wall. And his trousers had silver studs up the seam like a mini ladder – so I could climb without him even knowing I was there.

If only everyone wore clothes decorated with jewels, I thought as I swung up the pearl buttons of his shirt. It would make getting around much easier for little spies like me! (I kept well away from his open collar and all that chest hair, though. I could get lost in there for days!)

NASTY!

With one last leap, I swung off a button and
popped into the wide, bulging pocket
on the front of Barry's shirt.

I'd hoped I'd find the stolen
jewellery – probably the locket,
perhaps Mr Gupta's gold watch.
Or the twins' earrings. But there
was nothing in Barry's
pocket but a minty
breath freshener spray, a sachet of
orange fake tan and a
tube of FiXAGUM
tooth glue. Strange! What
did Barry want with

FIXAGUM? That was the glue Mrs Paterson used to keep her false teeth in place.

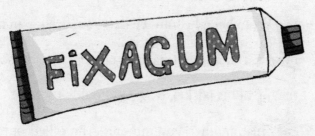

I peeked out of Barry's pocket and. . .

"Whoops!"

. . .I ducked down quick just as he stopped in front of the mirror to peer at himself again. If he looked down, he'd catch sight of me. He'd see me staring out of his pocket in his own reflection. I tried not to wriggle around too much either in case he felt me kicking against his chest.

V - E - R - Y   s - l - o - w - l - y, I tipped my head back, resting my cheek on the packet of fake tan like a pillow.

"Perfect!"

From here, I could see Barry's reflection in the mirror. But I didn't have to poke my head above the top of his pocket. So Barry couldn't see me.

"Just another few minutes!" he called out to the twins, who were still turned away from him under their dryers.

This is it, I thought. *Any second now he's going to steal something from them . . . and I'll be right here to see it!*

But Barry didn't move from in front of the mirror. Instead, he did the strangest thing I have ever seen. . . He glanced over his shoulder one last time to check no one was looking . . . then he lifted his hair clean off the top of his head!

"YIKES!"

His long blond curls were nothing but a wig! Underneath it, Barry Bling was as bald as a boiled egg!

CHAPTER 23

"Ha!" I know it's mean, but a little giggle built up inside me.

No wonder Barry only ever scratches the hair on his chest, I thought. *The hair on his head isn't real!*

As he stepped back from the mirror, I risked poking my head out of his pocket to see what he was going to do next. He stroked the wig as if it were a pet cat. Then he laid it down on top of the chest of drawers.

"Still nice and warm?" he called to the twins who were under their hairdryer hoods with their backs to him.

If only I could get down and investigate the wig closer. I was sure there was something suspicious about it. Otherwise, why would Barry risk taking it off in Cora and Dora's room? It just didn't make sense for someone so vain. But it wasn't going to be easy to climb out of Barry's pocket without him seeing me.

I'd have to be quick. I looked down at the fluffy blond curls lying on top of the drawers beneath me. The wig would make a lovely soft landing. Time for my most daring jump yet. I heaved myself up in Barry's pocket. I balanced my feet on the top of his minty mouth-freshener spray and leapt into space. . .

I somersaulted TWICE in mid-air, like I'd done a million times

on my best friend Nisha's trampoline ... and
landed safely in the
curls of the wig.

"Ouch!" The bed
of hair wasn't half as
soft as I'd expected;
something hard and pointy dug into my back.

Barry glanced down. I **froze** – sure that he'd
seen me amongst the curls. But his hand shot past
me to the two jewellery boxes beside the wig.

"Nice!" whistled Barry under his breath. He
took a silver bracelet from each box and stood for a
moment, weighing them in his hands.

"If you've got anything precious, ladies, make
sure you keep it locked up with all this horrible
thieving going on!" he shouted to the twins.

"You can't be too careful!"

"Thank you! You are kind to look after us!" called back Cora from under her dryer.

Anger shot through me like a bolt of lightning.

How could Barry get away with this? As usual, he was pretending to be Mr Nicey-Nice!

"We don't own anything precious, Barry dear," hollered Cora. "Not since our earrings were stolen. We've just got a couple of old bracelets our father gave us when we were girls. They mean the world to us, of course. But they're not worth any money."

"They're not even *real* silver," chipped in Dora.

Behind their backs, Barry's bald head wrinkled into a frown. Then he shrugged and kept hold of the bracelets anyway.

"I expect they're quite old now," he said. "You never know how much things like that might be worth."

"Thief!" I cried, but no one heard me.

Barry Bling might be a horrible person – picking on little old ladies who don't have much money and can't protect themselves – but he was horribly clever, too!

Here he was, slithering about, stealing from lovely old Cora and Dora while they were RIGHT HERE! In the same room! Under a hairdryer hood. . . It was like Mrs Paterson and the cucumber slices all over again.

"Cora! Dora!" I cried. But it was no use.

If I didn't stop Barry, no one would ever realize he was the thief.

The first thing I needed to do was investigate the wig. I was just about to peek underneath it when Barry leant down and stroked it with his fingers. His hand was so close it almost brushed against me. Not daring to move, I stared at his nearest ring. It was a big grinning skull with twinkly diamond eyes. I slipped behind a roll of curls and shuddered. With those fat fingers, Barry could squash me in a second. I had a nasty feeling he wouldn't think twice about stopping anybody who got in his way. I'd been crazy to make so much noise and risk being seen. If I wanted to prove that Barry was the thief, I mustn't let him catch me first.

I scampered out of sight, ducking behind the D for Dora jewellery box.

"A couple more minutes under those dryers and you'll be done, ladies," Barry called.

Taking care to stay hidden, I peeked round the edge of the box, poking my head out as if I were playing a scary game of hide-and-seek.

Barry took hold of the wig and flipped it over.

"WOW!" In spite of everything, a tiny gasp escaped me. I couldn't believe what I saw. Barry Bling's wig was FULL of jewellery!

It sparkled like a wicked pirate's hoard of treasure. There were necklaces, earrings, bracelets and Mr Gupta's gold watch – everything that had been stolen from the old people was there. It looked as if Barry hadn't even sold anything yet. He was probably waiting for the fuss to die down.

I shivered, realizing again how horribly clever he had been. Mrs Paterson's diamond ring had been found when the nurses searched Gran's room. But if anyone searched Barry's beauty case, or even his flat, they wouldn't find a thing.

All the jewellery Barry had stolen was in the very last place anyone would EVER think to look. It was shimmering and glimmering, safe inside his wig.

CHAPTER 24

I tiptoed further forward and peered round the edge of a photo frame.

I thought about what Barry had told Mrs Paterson on the veranda earlier.

"Wearing precious jewels is the very best way to keep them safe," he'd said.

…And here he was with a whole hoard of goodies hidden away inside a secret wig nobody even knew he wore. It must have been pretty uncomfortable when it was on his head. I remembered the hard lump when I'd landed on the wig. And I was surprised everything didn't fall out. . .

But then I saw what Barry was up to. He had taken the tube of **FIXAGUM** false-teeth glue out of his pocket. He was working quickly, beads of sweat shining on his bald head as he squeezed a blob of **FIXAGUM** on to the inside of the wig. He reached into his trouser pocket and pulled out the gold locket he'd stolen from Mrs Paterson on the veranda. Barry stuck the locket into the blob of glue.

So that's what the **FIXAGUM** was for! Barry stuck the jewellery inside his wig so that nothing would fall out when he was wearing it. Mrs Paterson had said **FIXAGUM** was strong enough to hold her false teeth in place even if she chewed on a **REALLY** sticky toffee. It must be strong enough to hold the jewellery steady too.

"Nearly ready, ladies," Barry called, looking towards the twins underneath their dryers.

The minute his head was turned, I stuck my hand out to test the glue. I don't know why I did it. It was like the time my Uncle Dan took me swimming at the seaside. I touched a jellyfish, just to see if it would sting me. (It did!) It was the same with the glue. There it was, oozing all around the locket. I just *had* to know how sticky it was.

It turns out ... it was VERY STICKY. The minute my tiny fingers touched the glue, I couldn't move them any more. I was stuck to the inside of the wig!

Barry turned back to the mirror. He lifted the

wig (and me!) on to his head.

As soon as his wig was back on, Barry glanced at himself in the mirror. Then he hurried over to turn the dryers off. If he'd looked any closer, he'd have seen my tiny face peering out from under his fringe. With shaking fingers, I quickly pulled a curl over my head with my one free hand. The other hand was still stuck down in the glue. Now that my whole body was squashed inside the wig, my legs, back and bum were stuck solid too.

"All done!" said Barry. He released the twins from their space helmet dryers. "You both look gorgeous," he said, fluffing up their hair. "Could one of you *lovely* ladies be a darling and pop out to the veranda for me? Tell Mrs Paterson I'll be out to take off her face mask in a moment.

I've got a little job to do first."

What was he up to now? The nicer Barry pretended to be, the more I hated him! How could he fool people so easily? The kind old twins trusted him. Mrs Paterson trusted him. So did Nurse Bridget . . . even Gran.

"Thank you, my dears!" Barry blew them a kiss, then sped out of the bedroom door with me stuck helplessly inside his wig.

Where's he off to in such a hurry? I thought. I glanced hopelessly from side to side. Although my body was stuck solid, my little head bobbed up and down underneath his fringe, poking out like a face from a sleeping bag.

Then Barry skidded to a stop . . . right outside Gran's room!

What was he doing here? My chest thumped. Gran wouldn't have ordered a beauty treatment. Not when she was so worried about the jewellery thefts.

"Mrs Short," he whispered, opening the door. "Are you in?"

Gran's bedside light was on but she was still under the covers. Not even her head was poking out.

"Are you awake?" whispered Barry.

Gran didn't answer.

"I've brought you a nice packet of face mask," Barry said, tiptoeing across the room. "It's Egyptian Nile mud. . . I'll just put it here, on your dressing table. Mud is very soothing if you're worried and stressed."

Gran still didn't say a word.

Peeping out from under Barry's fringe, I saw him place the face mask on the edge of Gran's dressing table.

"Phew!" It was getting hot under this wig. I was trying to blink the sweat out of my eyes when I froze. Barry was still holding the two silver bracelets he'd taken from Cora and Dora. Of course! He'd never put them under his wig.

He dangled them in the air for a moment, then dropped the two small, silver chains into the WORLD'S BEST GRANNY mug. Exactly the same place that the stolen diamond ring had been found.

"Stop!" My voice was muffled as I wriggled inside the wig, trying to kick my tiny glued-down feet against Barry's big bald head. I didn't care if he caught me now. So much the better! Gran would wake up and we could stop him together. "Take those bracelets back!"

I knew what Barry was doing! He didn't want to keep the bracelets for himself. He knew they weren't valuable. But if he left them in Gran's room, everyone would be even more sure that she was the thief!

"Don't you dare do this, Barry Bling!" I wriggled around like a glued-down caterpillar, pounding at his forehead with my one free hand.

"**Ahhh!**" Barry leapt about two metres in the air. He began madly scratching his head. "Help!" he cried. "Help! I've got nits."

Gran sat up in bed.

"Barry? What are you doing here? Whatever is the matter?" she gasped.

"Nits!" cried Barry again. "I can feel them nibbling under my hair."

"*Under* your hair?" said Gran.

"*In* my hair," said Barry, trying to sound calmer. "I mean, *in* my hair. This is all Violet's fault! I told you she was infested with nits. Now she passed them on to me!"

"I haven't got nits!" I hissed, w^riggli^ng even more.

"But I'm going to act like a nit. I'm going to make you itch and itch, Barry Bling!"

"Come here, Barry," said Gran, swinging her legs out of bed and turning on the main light. "Bend down. I'll have a look in your hair."

"No!" Barry leapt across to the other side of

the room ... probably remembering that his hair wasn't hair at all. It was a wig. And it was full of stolen jewellery!

"Don't be such a baby!" Gran grabbed a comb off her bedside table. "Come on!"

"I'm fine!" Barry tried to dodge sideways. But Gran was after him. She'd had plenty of practice at trying to catch me when I didn't want to comb my hair.

"Come on! I'll just have a look," she said.

"Please don't!" begged Barry, trying a new approach. "I'm too embarrassed."

I wriggled my legs again and he began to scratch like mad.

The more I wriggled, the more he itched. I couldn't help it. I began to laugh.

"Oh dear!"

My whole body was shaking now. The thought of Barry Bling the Big **BAD** jewellery thief getting in such a state because he thought he had nits *in his wig* was just too much for me!

And then...

wHOOSH!

The next thing I knew I'd shot back to **FULL SIZE**. Tears of laughter were streaming down my face.

I looked down and saw that I was sitting right on top of bald-headed Barry. He was pinned to the ground underneath me. I'd broken free of the glue when I had grown. But there I was. Still in my pyjamas ... with Barry's wig resting, lopsided, on the top of my head!

"What? ... How? ... Where did you come from?" he gasped.

But I just grinned.

"Got you, thief!" I said. "You're under arrest, Barry Bling!"

CHAPTER 25

A week later, Gran and I stood in the queue to ride PLUNGER!

Gran was grinning from ear to ear and wearing her favourite rainbow-striped top.

Mum was worried Gran shouldn't go on the ride, but Nurse Bridget had checked that it was OK for old people. As long as they didn't have a heart condition, it was fine.

Cora, Dora and Mr Gupta were all giving it a go too. And Nurse Bridget. They were giggling like schoolchildren in the queue behind me.

"It is **VERY** tall!" said Cora.

"Huge!" agreed Dora.

I was trying hard not to get too excited! After all, I didn't want to shrink before I was measured for the ride.

But I couldn't help it.

"This is TOTALLY, TOTALLY brilliant!" I cried, flinging my arms in the air and nearly bopping poor old Mr Gupta in the face.

"Quite right! You enjoy it, my dear!" he said.

"Yes," agreed Cora smiling and wrinkling up her freckled nose. "This is your treat, Violet. After all, you are the one who solved the mystery of the jewellery thefts."

"Not that I'll ever understand quite how you worked it all out!" said Dora.

"Oh, it was easy, really," I shrugged.

"Violet just followed a few tiny little clues!" giggled Gran.

We'd decided it was best not to try and explain too much.

"Shrinking is a tricky business," Gran had reminded me. "The world may not be ready for

your little talent quite yet!"

"*Our* little talent," I had smiled. "Don't forget, you were a shrinker too!"

In the end, we didn't need to explain much anyway. As soon as Nurse Bridget saw Barry's wig stuffed full of jewels, she called the police. They took Barry away and it was *him* who had to answer all the questions. It turns out the police were already looking for him.

Barry used to work as a groomer in a poodle parlour. (That's when all his hair fell out. He had an allergic reaction to dog fleas. No wonder he didn't want to catch nits!) But last Christmas, he ran away with all the money the poodle parlour had raised for a lost dog charity called PAW THINGS. I always knew Barry was mean ... but stealing money from puppies is just plain horrible!

"You did a good job, Violet," said Mr Gupta as we shuffled forward in the PLUNGER! queue. He handed me a mint humbug.

"Thank you!" I slipped the sweet into my pocket with the four others he'd given me already. I hadn't opened any of them. I'd been offered fizzy drinks and junk food too, but I'd turned them all down. Instead, I'd brought along a packet of dry, BORING Oaty Flakes to munch.

"At least Barry will be properly punished now!" said Nurse Bridget.

"It would be punishment enough to have to go on *that* thing," said Mrs Paterson, staring up at PLUNGER! She was with us in the queue but wasn't actually going to ride.

"Because of my weak heart!" she explained. "Also, I'd worry that when I turned upside down on the roller coaster, my false teeth would fly out! I can't find my tube of FIXAGUM anywhere!"

"Oh dear! I think Barry might have stolen that too!" I said.

"Honestly!" sighed Mr Gupta. "Is there

NOTHING that man wouldn't pinch?"

"Maybe I should wait with you while the others go on the ride, Nan," said Riley. Mrs Paterson had insisted that he come along on the trip. But from the nervous way he was nibbling his fingernails, he didn't seem very thrilled to have been invited.

"I mean, just so you don't get lonely," he said,

breathing deeply and clutching his stomach.

"I – er – don't mind missing my go. If I have
to . . . I'm not scared or anything." He shot a look
at me. "I'm not going to run away like *some* people
did!"

I wasn't so sure. It looked to me like Riley was
ready to scuttle off any second.

"You're such a kind boy," said Mrs Paterson.

"But don't worry, Riley. I'll just wait at the side there. You enjoy the ride."

"Er ... OK! Er ... thanks," breathed Riley, gulping for air. He looked so nervous now his cheeks were puffed up like a hamster. He didn't look so much like a rat any more. More like Hannibal! (Who, I'm pleased to say, was found safe and sound in the store cupboard at Sunset. He was chewing his way through a stack of spare toilet rolls.)

"Is this queue *ever* going to move?" groaned Tiffany, who was standing behind Riley.

I don't know why Gran had to be nice and offer to bring her along either! Tiffany doesn't even *like* theme parks. And it's not like *she* helped solve the great jewellery robbery.

"Actually, the queue is moving quite quickly!"
I pointed ahead of us. "Look! We're nearly at the measuring point already!"

I stuffed another handful of Oaty Flakes into my mouth.

But just as Tiffany looked up, there was a horrible retching sound and Riley threw up. SPLAT.... all over her new, blue high-heeled shoes.

"YUCK!" Tiffany screamed and ran to the toilets.

"I hope there's not a rat in there any more," I giggled.

"Sorry! BLUUURRRRR! Nerves!" puked Riley again. He ran to the toilets too.

"My poor poppet!" cried Mrs Paterson. She ran after Riley.

"Should I go and check on Tiff as well?" said Gran.

"No!" I squeezed her hand. "You'll miss the ride. Look!"

I stared at the sign just ahead of us.

PLUNGER

▶1.4ₘ
HEIGHT RESTRICTION
YOU MUST BE AT LEAST AS TALL AS THIS LINE
TO RIDE!

"And I *am* one point four metres tall!" I whispered, stuffing handfuls of Oaty Flakes into my mouth. "I am UTTERLY, TOTALLY, EXACTLY one point four metres tall."

"Why are you still eating that stuff?" whispered Gran, looking down at my cereal packet. "I thought it was excitement, not Oaty Flakes, that makes you shrink."

"*Exactly!*" I whispered back. "I don't *want* to shrink today! I want to stay FULL SIZE. I want to be exactly one point four metres tall so I can ride on PLUNGER!"

"Ah!" said Gran. "But I still don't understand about the cereal?"

"It's all part of my latest BRILLIANT plan!" I explained. "I mustn't get overexcited. So I'm just going to keep chewing the Oaty Flakes and thinking about how BORING they taste! So long as I keep stuffing them in my mouth, there's a chance I might not shrink!"

"BRILLIANT!" agreed Gran. "TOTALLY BRILLIANT!"

"This is SO exciting!" giggled Cora and Dora behind us.

"A thrill indeed!" agreed Mr Gupta.

I closed my eyes and tried to imagine all the most boring things I could think of: spelling tests, traffic jams, Tiffany trying to decide which top to wear. . .

"Next," called a theme park man in a yellow jacket. "Step up to the measuring line, please. Are you tall enough to ride on PLUNGER!, little girl?"

Who was he calling LITTLE?

"I AM TOTALLY, TOTALLY ONE POINT FOUR METRES TALL..."

It is really *very* hard not to get overexcited on the BIGGEST and BEST day of your WHOLE life ... I stuffed another handful of boring Oaty Flakes in my mouth.

"Here goes!" I said.

But as I stepped forward, I felt a tiny, tiny tingling in my toes...

Acknowledgements

Huge thanks to Sophie McKenzie for many readings, wise words and biscuits. Also Pat White and Claire Wilson at RCW for support and knowledge. To Polly Nolan for the spark. To all the team at Scholastic. And Alice Swan for editing with joy!

LOOK OUT
for Violet's other adventures

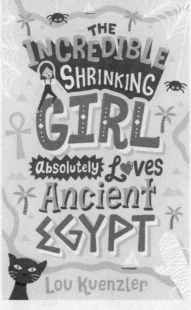

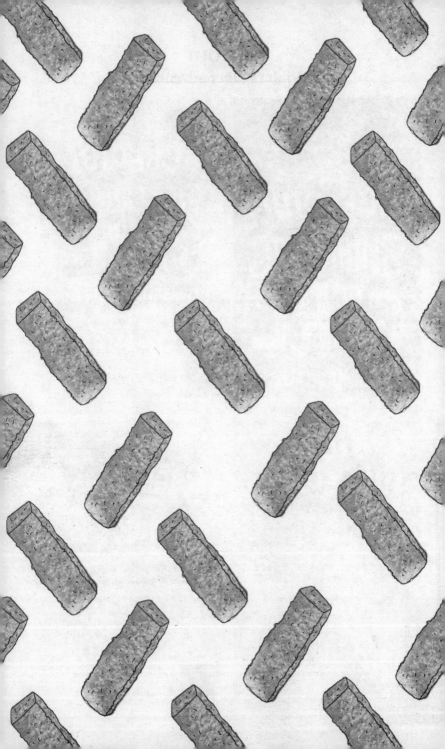